THE SHADOW GUARD

A SECOND GUARD NOVEL

THE
SHADOW
GUARD

A SECOND GUARD NOVEL

BY J. D. VAUGHN

DISNEY · HYPERION
LOS ANGELES   NEW YORK

Printed in the United States of America
FAC-020093-16166
First Edition, September 2016
1 3 5 7 9 10 8 6 4 2

Library of Congress Cataloging-in-Publication Data
Names: Vaughn, J. D., author.
Title: The shadow guard / by J. D. Vaughn.
Description: First edition. | New York ; Los Angeles : Disney-Hyperion,
[2016] | Series: A second guard novel | Summary: When the Earth guild
begins to demand fairer treatment by the queen, Brindl Tacora, an Earth
guilder and now Master of Messages for the Princess, must choose sides:
join the rebellion, or stay loyal to the crown.
Identifiers: LCCN 2015045250 | ISBN 9781423170976 (hardback)
Subjects: | CYAC: Fantasy. | Kings, queens, rulers, etc.—Fiction. |
Insurgency—Fiction. | BISAC: JUVENILE FICTION / Action &
Adventure / General. | JUVENILE FICTION / Legends, Myths, Fables /
General. | JUVENILE FICTION / Love & Romance.
Classification: LCC PZ7.V4655 Sh 2016 | DDC [Fic]—dc23
LC record available at http://lccn.loc.gov/2015045250

Visit www.DisneyBooks.com

SUSTAINABLE Certified Sourcing
FORESTRY
INITIATIVE www.sfiprogram.org
SFI-00993

THIS LABEL APPLIES TO TEXT STOCK

FOR FIRST-BORN COLE ZIMMER
AND SECOND-BORN RYAN DURANGO,
WITH LOVE AND MORE LOVE
AND YOUR FAVORITE MEALS

Under no circumstances shall a servant approach a Royal without permission from a Palace Court attendant.

—CH. N. TASCA, *Palace Etiquette*

ONE

he second Brindl registered the frayed rope, the wrought-iron chandelier, and the princess sitting beneath it, her body moved of its own accord.

Run! the voice inside her head commanded, though she was halfway across the drawing room by then.

Princess Xiomara sat with her back to Brindl and her head down, studying the parchments that lay on the desk in front of her, oblivious to the impending danger. Her dark hair hung unadorned, cascading down the simple white gown that was her preferred uniform.

"Princess!" Brindl yelled, as the rope snapped above them.

Brindl dove toward Xiomara, grabbed her by the

shoulders, and pulled her under the heavy wooden desk.

CRASH!

Brindl held her breath as the tabletop splintered underneath the massive weight of the chandelier. Please hold, please hold, please hold, she thought, covering Xiomara's body with her own and folding her arms over the princess's head for extra protection.

The desk groaned and cracked, but the sturdy, solid oak legs held.

Brindl let out a long sigh and slowly released the princess. "Many pardons, Your Highness. I hope you're not hurt?"

The princess had buried her face in her hands and now let out a few muffled sobs.

Brindl tilted her head and raised her eyebrows.

The princess continued to sniffle, her shoulders shaking at the fright she'd just received.

"But you're not the princess, are you?" Brindl asked, though she already knew the answer. Princess Xiomara was not one to sniffle.

The young woman shook her head and dropped her hands from her face. "No," she said, wiping her tears.

Of course, Brindl realized. It was Layna, lady's maid to Princess Xiomara. The two often dressed in the same simple style of the Moon Guild. From behind they looked nearly identical.

"Forgive me, Lady Layna," Brindl said, pulling the trembling young woman from beneath the desk. "Mind your head—"

"What in Elia's name happened here?" interrupted a voice from behind them.

Zarif. Brindl would know that refined voice anywhere, though she rarely saw its owner. In fact, she rarely saw any of her old Alcazar friends since they had been assigned to Xiomara's service in the royal city three moons ago.

"The rope . . . it was frayed," began Brindl, trying to compose herself before meeting his gaze. She and Zarif had been close once, but that seemed like a lifetime ago. Now with Zarif installed as Xiomara's counselor, and Brindl as Master of Messages, the two of them had agreed early on to put a halt to their relationship. There were rules in the palace, *strict* rules, especially for lady servants such as Brindl. And Zarif's service to Princess Xiomara, Tequende's Queen-in-Waiting, was far more important than the feelings they'd once shared. Brindl understood that.

Still, she missed him.

Zarif frowned at the rope, which now lay across the floor, then turned his attention to Layna. "You've obviously had quite a scare," he said, taking her by the elbow.

"I'll be fine," she whispered, though her face remained pale, nearly matching her gown. "Had Brindl not arrived when she did—" Her voice began to quiver and she blinked back more tears. "Had she not pulled me beneath the desk—"

Zarif nodded, then glanced at Brindl. "It sounds like Brindl arrived just in time, thank the Gods."

By then, several palace servants and guards had entered the room to investigate the loud crash. Brindl watched Zarif take command of the growing crowd as though born to lead, despite the crutches and amputated leg he'd suffered not long ago. "Escort Lady Layna back to her quarters, please," Zarif ordered, directing his comments to two maids. "The rest of you can clear this mess. And summon the chamberlain to have that chandelier restrung," he added, frowning again at the rope. "Tell her I'd like a word when she's done."

The assembled group murmured in assent, then quickly began to carry out the tasks. Brindl hesitated, unsure if she'd been included in Zarif's orders, though she hadn't yet carried out her own business. She cleared her throat behind him.

Zarif turned, and Brindl saw his face soften just the smallest bit. *He misses me, too,* she realized, watching him shake his head as if to clear it. *Though he works hard to overcome it.*

"Brindl, thank you for your quick actions today. You may well have saved Layna's life," he said, glancing at the debris. Three muscular guards now wrestled with the heavy, iron chandelier, trying to disengage it from the splintered desk. "How did you come to be here in Xiomara's drawing room?"

Brindl stuck a hand in the pocket of her tunic and pulled out a tiny scroll. "A message from the Queen's Sword. It's marked private, so I thought I'd deliver it myself. Doesn't the princess join you here in the afternoon?" she asked, trying to respond with equal formality.

"Yes, we usually review correspondence at this time, though today we were summoned to a meeting with the Queen. Xiomara sent Layna here in her stead to reply to some invitations."

"I see. Shall I leave this message with you, then?"

Zarif nodded and extended his palm.

Brindl dropped the small scroll into the elegant brown hand that had held hers so many times before. When she lifted her eyes to meet his, she found them already gazing at her, as if trying to read her thoughts.

"Very well," Brindl said with a slight curtsy. "I'll return to the aviary now if you have no need for me."

"You've helped enough today," he said. "You're free to go." As Brindl turned to leave, Zarif spoke again, lowering his voice. "I believe Tali and Chey are coming for tea in the library tonight at nine bells. Will you join us?"

Brindl's heart lifted. Finally, she would see her old friends.

"It would be my pleasure," she said, trying to keep the smile from her face.

"Until then," Zarif said, with a curt nod of dismissal.

"Until then," Brindl repeated, but Zarif had already turned his attention back to the work at hand.

As soon as Brindl entered the rooftop aviary, Pip began to chirp in excitement and flap his tiny wings. Brindl reached into the small cage and scooped up the baby bluejacket. She had named him Pip, for he was the runt of the flock, though what he lacked in size he more than made up for in pluckiness.

She stroked the bird's downy feathers, smiling at his contented coos. Pip loved to be held, and Brindl was pleased to oblige. "At least *you* look happy to see me each day," she said, tickling Pip's head with the tip of her fingernail.

Brindl carried him across the roof between towers and spires to the western edge of the palace. A wooden storage locker used to hold arrows and other weapons provided her a perfect perch from which to gaze over the stone battlement surrounding the roof.

As she seated herself on the trunk, a highland wind sent a shiver across her shoulders, but the spectacle in front of her was worth the risk of a cold. From here she could see the entire city of Fugaza laid before her like a tapestry.

The Sun God Intiq had just begun his descent toward the Sentry Hills, which encircled the city like a mother's arms. The Queen's Palace, hewn from the eastern ring of the hills, towered over the valley like an eagle guarding its nest. Down below, the great Magda River gurgled at the foot of the palace, providing a natural moat. A three-tiered bridge connected the palace grounds to the rest of the city, which bustled with activity. Buildings of every shape and size filled the valley, though they all shared the same white-washed walls, arched doorways, and caramel-colored roof tiles. Clean, cobbled roads ran through the city like ribbons, occasionally skirting bright green parks, sparkling blue fountains, or the numerous flower gardens that provided splashes of color in the city of white.

Compared to the humble village of Zipa where Brindl had been raised, the scene in front of her seemed almost pretend, as if from a whimsytale her grandfather once told her. *Though I should have expected no less of a city built by Moon Guilders*, she mused.

The thought of Moon Guilders made her crane her neck over the battlement to see if she might spot any of her friends on one of the balconies below. Empty. Only once had she seen Tali, Chey, and Zarif on the central balcony that jutted over the river. She'd been tempted to call down to them, and almost did so, when she remembered herself and swallowed her words. That was more than two weeks ago. She'd not caught a glimpse of them since.

Brindl tried to ignore the lump in her throat. "They're very busy, you see," she explained to Pip, who bobbed his head toward her, as if listening. "They have important jobs here at the palace and much to do."

Pip fluttered his wings and pecked gently at Brindl's fingers.

"Still, you'd think they could spare a moment to sit on the roof with us," Brindl added with a wistful smile. "Just look what they're missing."

She knew she should be happy—grateful even. Honored. Princess Xiomara, the Queen-in-Waiting of Tequende, had assigned Brindl to be her official Master of Messages. The title was merely a fancy term for pigeonkeep, but that was no matter. As a member of Xiomara's retinue, she'd been given her own quarters—her own *tower*, in fact—near the rooftop aviary. Wasn't it better to have her own lovely rooms, appointed with featherbed, desk, and a whole case of books, rather than be placed with all the other servant girls in the overcrowded, lower level of the palace near the raging river?

Brindl stifled a sigh. She loved her tower. She truly did. She enjoyed her quiet rooftop life, tending the baby birds, reading the books, and admiring the spectacular sunset every day. But the isolation from the other servants, and especially her old friends from the Alcazar, sometimes brought on a sudden wave of loneliness. She longed to exchange a laugh with them, to hear about their adventures in the palace below. At times it felt as if they'd forgotten her. And she ached for Saavedra, the old mentor who had taught her not only how to tend bluejackets, but how to think about the world in new ways.

And he would never allow you to wallow in this pity, she reminded herself.

She stood then, determined to concentrate on her new tasks and push the loneliness from her mind. Brindl stuck her pointer finger out to Pip, who stepped onto the perch, gripping it tightly with his tiny talons. As they strolled along the roof, Brindl raised her arm up and down, forcing the baby bird to extend his wings and practice gaining balance. Every few minutes she would reward him with honey-roasted seeds from her pocket.

She tried to spend at least a quarter hour daily with each of the fledglings this way. Although Saavedra had never tended baby birds during their work together at the Alcazar, he'd left meticulous notes about how to raise and train them. The breeding pair of bluejackets and twelve fledglings now in her care had been a gift from Villa del Norte, one of the realm's few aviaries spared the widespread bluejacket poisoning during the Battle for the Alcazar.

So many dead birds, Brindl thought, and Saavedra, too.

He had been gone nearly six moons now. As the days slid by, the pinch of grief had slowly been replaced by the warm memories she had of the man who had once been high counselor to the Queens of Tequende. *How he would love to see me here in Fugaza, working in the palace as he himself once did,* Brindl thought with a grin. *Even if I am just a pigeonkeep.*

The smile left her face as soon as she spied the tall, angular form of the chamberlain across the roof, striding purposefully in Brindl's direction.

"Oh no, Pip," murmured Brindl, tucking the bird into her apron pocket and smoothing her skirt. "What have I done now?"

As the chamberlain neared, Brindl braced herself for the lecture that was to come, for Nadea Tasca of the royal family did not open her thin-lipped mouth unless it was to give order or admonishment. Brindl feared the latter.

"Brindl Tacora!" she barked, her eyes sweeping Brindl up and down.

"Yes, Chamberlain." Brindl wondered how the woman could think straight with her hair pulled back so severely into a single oiled braid. *Maybe she's trying to smooth out her frown lines. Only it's not working.*

"Under whose orders did you deliver a message to the Queen-in-Waiting's private quarters this afternoon?"

Brindl cleared her throat. She knew from experience there would be no correct answer. "Under no one's orders, Chamberlain. As Xiomara's Master of Messages, I thought I should take it myself."

The chamberlain pressed her lips together, making her look even more peevish, if such a thing were possible. "You told me you could read, despite your Earth Guild upbringing. Were you lying?"

Brindl clinched her fists and tried to keep her face from flushing. "I was *not*, Chamberlain."

"Then exaggerating, perhaps, to gain your position here?"

Honestly, Brindl thought. I could kick her. She stood up straighter, though she still had to lift her chin to meet the tall woman's eyes, which galled her. "I did no such thing."

The chamberlain sniffed. "Perhaps you're just slow-witted then. I suggest you reread the copy of *Palace Etiquette* I gave you your first day here. I did not write that manual for it to be ignored. Queen Twenty-two herself commissioned it from me. Commit it to memory this time. In the future, you will request permission before you approach a Royal. Is that understood?"

"Yes, Chamberlain."

"And get that filthy bird out of your apron."

Brindl looked down to see Pip's head peeking out of her

apron. "Cheep CHEEP CHEEEEP!" the bird called loudly, as if in protest.

The chamberlain stiffened, then pivoted on one perfectly polished heel and walked briskly across the roof.

Brindl clapped a hand over her mouth to keep from laughing and scooped Pip out with the other. "You naughty thing," she whispered to the little bird. "Careful, or she'll throw us both from the roof, and you haven't got your wings yet."

Servants are strictly forbidden to engage socially with palace guards and attendants. All lady servants must report to their sleeping quarters by nine bells sharp each evening, unless otherwise instructed by the chamberlain.

—CH. N. TASCA, *Palace Etiquette*

TWO

rindl hesitated before the library door, unsure whether to knock first. The chamberlain's earlier reprimand had made her second-guess every move for the rest of the day, lest she be caught scratching her nose or walking on the wrong side of the hallway. Brindl glanced over her shoulder to make sure she wasn't being watched, then pushed the door open. She poked her head inside, relieved when she saw her three friends sitting at a far table.

As always, the Queen's Library gave her pause. The cavernous room towered three stories tall, with giant arched windows reflecting the candles and lanterns within. Thousands of volumes of books curved around the circular room, accessed by wooden staircases and balconies that wrapped themselves throughout the shelves like vines. Brindl almost felt dizzy gazing at the height and volume of books inside the chamber. How many lifetimes would it take to read so many books? she wondered, craning her neck to see them all.

"Brin!" a young man called, rising from his chair and smiling.

Brindl crossed the room and let Chey Maconde draw her into a fierce hug. Though she knew him for an Earth Guilder, he had shed all outward signs of his farm family upbringing and humble roots. He now wore the coveted uniform of the Second Guard, which hung handsomely from his broad frame, his once long hair trimmed closely to his tan face. He almost looks intimidating, Brindl thought, except that his eyes are still warm as a mug of chocolate.

"It's good to see you, friend," she said, returning his embrace.

"Thank Intiq you're finally here!" Tali interrupted, pulling Brindl into a nearby chair. "I thought I might be stuck with these two lugs all night."

Brindl laughed as Tali began to pour tea. The Second Guard uniform didn't fit Tali as nicely as it did Chey, too big in the arms and waist. Her hair had been pulled back in a single braid, like the chamberlain's, though several curled wisps had pulled loose around her face. Pretty as ever, Brindl decided, though she'd hate me to say so.

Zarif rose to assist Tali and turned to Brindl. "It's nice

to see you again, Brindl, under more pleasant circumstances this time."

"That's right, Brin, we heard you and Layna had quite a scare this afternoon," said Tali. "Good thing you noticed that frayed rope, Eagle Eye."

"Zarif says your swift action was nothing short of heroic," Chey agreed.

Brindl glanced at Zarif, trying to keep the blush from her cheeks. Zarif nodded, but did not meet her eyes. "So, Tali, what's this surprise you've been teasing us with?" he asked, pointing his chin to the box on the table.

Brindl wasn't sure whether to feel hurt or relieved by Zarif's swift change of subject. Though she didn't wish to dwell on the incident with the chandelier, she couldn't deny the pleasure she felt at being complimented by her friends. It had been so long since anything she'd done had received a kind word or recognition.

"I've brought the most magnificent treat," Tali said, reaching for the box and lifting the lid. "I scavenged it from the kitchens. Look, cake!"

The group leaned forward as Tali opened the box with a flourish, the sides dropping away to reveal a miniature masterpiece. For the cake was an exact replica of the palace itself, with every balustrade and balcony in its place. Even the giant windows looked real somehow, reflecting light in their candied incarnations.

"You scavenged this or stole it?" Zarif furrowed his brow at Tali, though his eyes betrayed amusement.

"I scavenged it fair and square, Zarif Baz Hasan," replied Tali, poking Zarif in the ribs. "Ask Chey if you don't believe me."

"It's true," Chey answered. "Tali's teaching the night cook's daughter how to spar. The girl's a second-born, off to the Alcazar in a few years. In exchange, the cook lets Tali raid the kitchens at will."

"Ah. That explains the plump cheeks," Zarif answered, raising a hand as if to pinch Tali's face, but she swatted it away.

"Don't listen to him, Tali," Brindl said. "You look like you could eat cake every night and still have room in that uniform. But this cake's too pretty to eat by half."

"Oh no it's not," said Tali, pulling a dagger from the holster in her boot.

Zarif grabbed her arm before she could start hacking away at the cake. "We're not eating in my library."

"*Your* library?" asked Tali. "I thought it was the Queen's Library. And since she never steps foot in here, why not?"

Brindl exchanged a look of amusement with Chey, while Zarif peered around nervously, as if Queen Twenty-two herself might be eavesdropping. Then he shook his head with a small laugh. "Sometimes I don't know if you're brave or stupid, Tali. Now if you'll turn the conversation to something less blasphemous, I'll get a proper knife and tablecloth for you heathens."

Brindl watched as Zarif left the room. He moved more quickly on his crutches now, and his lean body looked less frail. Most of the old vigor had returned to his face, Brindl decided, though it still pained her to see his pant leg pinned up where his missing leg should be. Tali and Chey had been gravely injured in battle as well, but their wounds were no longer visible, save a few scars. Together the two of them had kept Zarif alive in the Battle for the Alcazar, protecting his fallen body from certain death. Sometimes it seemed a lifetime ago, other times just a day. Brindl shivered in the drafty room.

"So how fares our Master of Messages?" Chey asked, leaning forward. The delicate teacup he held looked like a doll's toy in his large hands.

"As Saavedra used to say, I'm a humble pigeonkeep with a fancy title," Brindl answered, relaxing into her chair. "And how is your new position guarding the heir to the throne?"

Chey shrugged. "I can't complain. Though some days I feel more like a footstool than a soldier of the realm, to be honest."

"In other words, we do a lot of standing around," explained Tali. "So far the only threats to Xiomara have come from palace gossip and fawning suitors. Sometimes I'm so bored I actually miss our old training days at the Alcazar."

"Still, we should be grateful after all that's happened," said Chey. "I'd rather be bored than fighting for my life again."

The group sobered as their thoughts flew to that long night, when so many of their fellow pledges and comrades lost their lives. Chey rubbed his arm and Tali tugged on her own braid, as if grief had slipped into the empty chair beside them, solemn and gray.

Zarif returned then, a large basket hanging from one arm as he slowly maneuvered his way through the room on a single crutch.

Brindl leapt up at once. I should have gone with him, she scolded herself.

"Sit," Zarif commanded. "I'm fine."

Brindl sank back into the chair and stared at their reflection in the windows. Would they never be close again, the way they used to be?

"But would you please serve the cake for us, Brindl?" Zarif asked, his tone kinder this time. "If we leave it to Tali, we'll be wearing the cake instead of eating it."

Tali made a face at Zarif, and the mood lightened as Chey took a yellow tablecloth from the basket and spread it over the table.

Brindl scrutinized the cake, unsure how to slice it. "It

seems a shame to ruin it," she said, as Zarif handed her the knife. "I can't believe the cook let you have it, Tali. Surely it must have been made for a special occasion?"

Tali shook her head. "It's a practice cake. And trust me, it'll be even lovelier in our bellies."

"What do you mean it's a 'practice' cake?" Zarif asked, settling into the seat across from Brindl, as she reluctantly carved up the work of art.

Tali shrugged. "The cake makers like to experiment, I'm told. They're testing new designs and recipes to prepare for the upcoming Treaty Talks."

Once everyone was served, Chey immediately lifted his cake and took a huge bite from it. Crumbs spilled down his uniform like a star shower. Zarif shook his head and pointed at the forks.

"Fussy old Moon Guilder," Chey said, pulling up his chair, then grabbed a fork and winked at the girls.

The friends stopped talking as they ate, pausing only to let out a few appreciative grunts and sighs. "It's heavenly," Brindl finally said, after eating several bites. "Like long afternoons in the sun."

"The best thing I've ever tasted," Chey agreed, licking icing off his fingers, "save Nel's cooking, of course."

"Even my twin would agree this is food for the Gods," Tali answered.

"How is it that we have cake makers in Tequende anyway—isn't it a Far World delicacy?" Brindl asked.

"Who cares?" Tali stuffed another bite into her mouth. "As long as the cake makers keep baking."

Brindl and Zarif shook their heads and looked on as Tali and Chey fought for the last few crumbs in the cake box.

"Enjoy yourselves now, for when the regents come, I doubt the night cooks will be as generous with handouts," Zarif said. "The chamberlain has given strict orders for all palace staff and servants to be on their best behavior."

"So we've heard," replied Tali. "The Queen has decreed that her realm will 'sparkle like an emerald' so the regents can go back and tell their Far World masters what a jewel we are."

"Such folly—" began Brindl, then stopped herself. Palace servants were strictly forbidden to comment on royal matters, let alone question the Queen's orders. The chamberlain had made that more than clear.

Zarif gave her a look. "Go on, Brindl," he prompted. "You're among friends. Folly how?"

"Well . . . the Andorians and Castillians have nearly carved up the rest of the Nigh World for themselves. Tequende is one of the only native realms still standing. Why?" she asked, remembering how Saavedra used to prompt discussion by posing questions.

"Because until now we've had no gold," answered Zarif, playing along. "Our treasures lay in art and knowledge, commodities of little interest to Far World conquerors."

"Besides, we're too remote," added Chey, leaning back in his chair. "Our highlands are difficult to reach, not worth the trek for those seeking easy riches."

"*And* we have the Second Guard, the best-trained army in the Nigh World," said Tali, though she, like her friends, sounded more subdued than smug.

"Yet all that has changed now," said Brindl, giving voice to that which everyone at the table already knew. The Battle for the Alcazar. Not five moons ago, Jorge Telendor, the commander of the realm's army, had betrayed their Queen and nearly taken Tequende by force. His army of Oest Andorian mercenaries, funded by a hidden vein of gold deep within Tequende's salt mines, had laid siege to the Second Guard's island fortress, leaving hundreds of dead in its wake. The invaders would have succeeded, too, had it not been for Jaden Telendor, the commander's own son, and a brave group of tradeboaters, miners, and packhounds who turned the tide of the battle just when all was thought lost.

Zarif's eyes flickered down to the stump of his leg. "Much has altered within our realm, that is so," he agreed.

"And the Far World knows it," Brindl said. "Tequende has gold now. We were breached and nearly beaten. And the commander of our own army turned out to be a turncoat, which hardly speaks well for Queen Twenty-two . . . or the Second Guard," she added, with an apologetic look at her two uniformed friends.

"But Jaden is the Queen's Sword now," said Tali, her voice rising. "He's worked tirelessly to unify our forces, mend alliances, strengthen our border patrols these past several months. We've barely seen him, he's been so busy. The Second Guard will be—*is*—stronger than ever now."

Brindl nodded at her friend kindly. Tali kept her feelings for Jaden Telendor tucked deep inside, but Brindl knew they were there, however much Tali tried to hide them. "I know, Tali. I'm sure you're right."

"Still, your point is well taken, Brin," said Chey. "Our peaceful highlands are no longer so peaceful. Even worse, now we've turned the heads of the Far World monarchs, who once had little use for us."

Tali crossed her arms over her chest. "So let their regents sniff around us like dogs next month. They'll see we're not a people to be trifled with."

Zarif rubbed a hand down his cheek. "The Blood Queen of Andoria doesn't trifle with her enemies," he said quietly. "She kills them."

The room grew silent again.

"Perhaps our Queen means to trade in peace at the Treaty

Talks rather than riches," acknowledged Brindl, wishing it to be true.

"Let's hope so," said Chey, tidying up the empty plates and napkins. "I hate to end our party, but Tali and I must report back to Guard quarters now."

Tali licked the last bit of icing off her plate before passing it to him. "All the palace guards are on strict curfew these days. Larus, the Palace Centurio, has woken us every morning at five bells for the past week, quizzing us on every nook and cranny of this place. Did you know there are one hundred and eighty-seven rooms, not counting water closets and broom cupboards?" she asked Brindl. "And we're to memorize every door, every window, every balcony, every alcove where danger might lurk. Though if you ask me, the only danger in this palace is getting lost in it."

As Tali and Chey left the library, waving their good-byes, Brindl rose and took the basket from the table. "I'll return this, Zarif. I'm going to the kitchens anyway and—"

Zarif put up a hand. "No need to talk me into it, Brindl. I'm tired tonight and grateful for the offer, thank you. But before you go, may I have a quick word?"

Brindl set the basket back on the table. "Of course," she said, though her stomach turned over when she saw the somber look in his eyes.

"What made you notice the chandelier this afternoon?"

Brindl bit the inside of her cheek. *The voice told me.* But she couldn't tell Zarif that. She couldn't explain it without seeming crazy. "I'm not sure," she answered, avoiding his gaze. "I just happened to see the rope splitting, I guess."

"Ah," said Zarif, scratching his chin. "The rope. Chamberlain Tasca assures me the chandelier was freshly strung not two weeks ago. She herself inspected it. Yet when I examined the rope earlier, it almost looked as if it had been cut . . . as if someone had sliced the rope down to the last few fibers."

Brindl's head flew up. "Are you saying that someone cut the rope on purpose?"

Zarif sighed. "No. I don't know. I realize it seems far-fetched, but I can't come to any other logical explanation if the chamberlain is telling the truth. Did you happen to see anyone on your way to the drawing room earlier? Anyone at all?"

"I passed several palace servants in the hallways, but no one out of the ordinary," she said, trying to jog her memory. "There was a young man polishing the wall sconces outside the drawing room as I went in, though I didn't see his face."

"Did you notice any other details that might identify him? I'd like to speak with the man if I could."

Brindl shook her head. "He wore the same servant uniform as everyone else. His hair short, black . . . again, same as most. Average build." Brindl closed her eyes and tried to retrieve the image from her memory. She could see the shape of him in her mind, the stiff way he held himself, the methodical back and forth of his polishing rag. But nothing that would help place him. "I'm sorry, Zarif. Perhaps you could ask the chamberlain? She would know who was assigned to polish the sconces today. That woman knows everything," she added, unable to keep the irritation from her voice.

"Indeed she does," replied Zarif, grinning. "Good idea. I'll ask her."

Brindl nodded and reluctantly took the basket. She wished Zarif would ask her to stay. Spending an hour in the company of her old friends made her miss them more than ever. "Is there anything else I can help you with?"

"No thank you. Good night, Brindl."

Brindl tried not to let her shoulders fall. "Good night, Zarif."

The palace village exists to serve the Queen and her guests. Villagers should never be allowed to enter the palace unless necessary, and directly ordered to do so by the chamberlain.

—CH. N. TASCA, *Palace Etiquette*

THREE

rindl stepped out of her small tower just as Intiq peeked out from the clouds. She turned her face toward the warmth, grateful for the comforting rays after several days of rain, which had kept her cooped inside since her visit to the library. This is how the bluejackets must feel when I open their cage doors, she thought, stretching under the vast blue sky.

At home in Zipa, Brindl and her family had always worked well below the earth inside the complex world of salt mining. Weather was never an issue, good or bad. But here in the high hills of Fugaza, the damp, chilly air, which gusted across the palace roof, always seemed coldest in the mornings. This particular morning was an exception, and Brindl paused to give the Sun God an appreciative smile.

As she entered the aviary, the fourteen birds in her care chirped and rustled expectantly. "Soon enough, little birds, you'll each have your chance to fly," she said, filling the empty feed tins one at a time. "But for now you must eat and grow strong." As she scooped the last of the grain from the bin by the door, only a few dusty crumbs remained, making her sneeze. She stared at the empty container, wondering what to do next. The bin had been full when she'd taken over as pigeonkeep. No one had told her what to do when the grain ran out.

"Find the grainery, I suppose," Brindl said to the birds, "before you get hungry for dinner."

After she'd let out each bird to spread its wings in the fresh air, Brindl tucked the last one into its cage with a pat, then grabbed a bucket and left the sanctuary of her rooftop. She took several staircases down to the lower level of the palace, where she knew of at least one door by the kitchens that would take her to the outer grounds. As she turned down the final hallway, Brindl came to an abrupt halt. A half-dozen servants were polishing the parquet flooring, the tiles still damp with their work.

"Oh!" Brindl said, looking down at the wax she'd just marred.

"Must you come this way?" one of the servants asked, a polite smile plastered to her face, though Brindl could see the exasperation in her eyes.

"I suppose I could try another way, it's just that I'm not familiar—"

"Never mind," the maidservant answered. "Pass now, but quickly please."

"Truly, I am sorry for the inconvenience," Brindl said, scurrying on tiptoes across the floor, the bucket clanging against her legs.

Can I do nothing right in this place?

When she had first arrived, she had tried to engage in conversation with the other palace servants, but more often than not she had felt their response to be cool and distant. Whether this was due to her Earth Guild status or the chamberlain's strict rules about proper behavior, she was unsure. Both perhaps. In any case, after the first month, she'd learned to stay out of their way, taking her meals in the tower and keeping to herself.

As soon as she was outside the palace, she stopped to let out a long breath, as if she'd been holding it for weeks. She looked around and felt a sudden rush of joy. The palace village, with its many outbuildings, animals, and bustling Earth Guilders, almost reminded her of Zipa. Even the ground itself was a comfort, the damp springy grass a luxury beneath her slippers instead of the graveled pebbles of the rooftop.

She began walking through the bustle, smiling to herself as she did so. Though she had missed the feel of the Earth

Goddess Machué beneath her feet these past few months, more than that, she realized, she had missed the presence of people. *Her* people. Inside the palace walls, most servants were born and raised Moon Guilders, quiet and orderly in their countenance, neat to a fault in their spotless white uniforms. Out here, the servants wore the garb of the Earth Guilders back home—tunics, trousers, and skirts of browns and greens, their long hair left loose to swing at their shoulders or tied simply with string. Though they hurried along with their tasks, they seemed cheerful while doing so, calling greetings to one another or sharing snatches of news and gossip.

Brindl stepped aside to allow a woman pushing a handcart of maize to pass by. "May Machué bless you!" the woman called, as the small girl toddling beside her did the same. "Bess you!" the tot sang.

Brindl paused to look around and find her bearings. So many buildings! The white structures all looked alike to her, scattered among the green hillside like giant cubes of sugar. She shook her head to think that this entire village—every stable, every shed, every outbuilding—existed for the sole purpose of serving the Queen and her palace. Just like the Alcazar, she thought, remembering the fortress where she had been assigned as a second-born servant last year. Only prettier, she decided.

A young boy scurried past then, a handful of mountain berries spilling from his pail.

"Excuse me, which way to the grainery, please?" Brindl asked him, bending to collect the fallen berries.

"Left at the tailor's, right at the spinner house," the boy replied, barely slowing down. "Keep them!" he added with a wave, as Brindl reached out to return the berries to his pail.

Brindl blew the dust off the fruit and popped them past her parched lips. The explosion of juice filled her mouth and she sighed deeply again, happy to have escaped her tower for a short time. She would have to find reasons to come outside more often.

The clank of hammer on steel grew louder as Brindl passed the smith, pulling her out of her thoughts. Left at the tailor's, right at the spinner house, she said to herself, trying to figure out which building was which. Some of them were obvious. Alpacas poked their funny faces out of the windows of a nearby shed, vying for a chance to be fed scraps. Brindl could not resist scratching a baby one behind the ears, much to his delight. The next building housed a brood of chickens, squawking and complaining as one by one their eggs were stolen by two young girls.

As she came to a small intersection of walkways, Brindl pivoted in a circle, searching for anything that might resemble the tailor's shop. Surprised by a voice behind her, Brindl turned and faced a young man about her age, wearing an apron over his simple clothes. His friendly eyes sparkled in a face that was golden brown like a native Tequendian, yet sharply angled and foreign somehow.

"Lost?" he asked, smiling.

"Quite lost I'm afraid."

"Where do you need to go?"

"The grainery," Brindl replied, lifting the pail on her arm as if offering proof. She immediately felt silly. *This is what happens when you talk to no one but birds all day,* she scolded herself.

"You're in luck. I'm going to the mill, which is right next door. We can walk together."

"Thank you. I'm Brindl Tacora of the Zipa Salt Miners," she said, offering her palm to him in the traditional greeting.

"Tonio Rossi of the Palace Bakers," he answered, placing his hand on hers. "You're far from home," he continued, as they began to walk. "Here for your second-born service to the Queen, I gather. Kitchens?"

Brindl tried not to be offended by his remark. It was a logical guess, of course. Under the Oath of Tequende, every second-born child of the realm upon reaching the age of fifteen was either sworn to six years of servant duty to the Queen or four years of Second Guard service. The vast majority of female Earth Guilders usually wound up as stable girls, scullery maids, or kitchen help.

Brindl shook her head. "I'm the pigeonkeep for Princess

Xiomara," she answered, lifting the pail again. "We seem to have run out of food."

"Pigeonkeep? That sounds like an interesting job," he said. "But I thought the bluejackets had all been killed by Telendor's men."

"Most of them were," admitted Brindl, her voice quieting. It still pained her to think of that day. "But we're breeding new ones. I have twelve little chicks in my charge now."

"So you're the mama bird," Tonio said, bringing a smile to her face. It was not hard to like this baker boy. He had an open, comfortable way about him that put her at ease. "How did you come to be a pigeonkeep? Forgive my ignorance, but I don't see how you could learn much about bluejackets down in the mines."

"No, not in the mines. When I reported to the Alcazar last year, I was placed in the service of the pigeonkeep there."

"You must have learned quickly if they chose you to serve the princess after only a year of training."

Brindl hesitated, unsure whether to explain the circumstances that had brought her to Fugaza.

Tonio noticed her discomfort. "If you were at the Alcazar last year, you must have been there for the battle," he said, his voice now solemn.

Brindl pressed her lips together. "I was."

Tonio nodded. They walked for a time in silence.

"Princess Xiomara asked my friends and me to serve her after we had won," Brindl finally said, suddenly wanting—needing—to explain herself. "We had all been friends with her former tutor, Manuel de Saavedra. I'm sure you've heard of him. He was counselor to the past three Queens, a brilliant man. He's the one who taught me how to pigeonkeep." Brindl stopped then, aware she hadn't spoken so many words in a row for a long while.

"My father used to read Saavedra's history book to me at night," Tonio said. "Lucky you to learn from such a man. And your friends, they are pigeonkeeps, too?"

Brindl let out a small chuckle. "Not in the slightest. Tali and Chey are personal guards to the princess. Zarif is her advisor and librarian."

Tonio raised his eyebrows. "Your friends are very important people, I see."

"Oh, yes, and they're kept quite busy," Brindl said, abruptly ready to talk about something else. "Have you always lived here in Fugaza?"

"I have, though my father came from the Far World," Tonio said. "Fiorenze."

So she had been right about his foreign features. Handsome, but different.

"In fact, he's the one who brought the Fiorenzan

cake-making tradition to Tequende," Tonio continued. "My mother and I bake cakes for the palace."

"Cake? I have tasted one of your amazing cakes! It was a practice one they said."

"Did they feed it to your bluejackets?" Tonio joked.

"No, no, of course not! I met with my friends the other night and Tali brought the most exquisite cake. It looked just like the palace!"

"Ah, that one. I'm glad someone enjoyed it. We've been trying to perfect the icing to be as stable as it is delicious."

"It was certainly delicious."

Tonio nodded, seemingly pleased by her enthusiasm. "The grainery," he said then, stopping in front of a white building that looked just like the others. "Stop by the bakery when you're done and I'll give you a slice of cake fresh from the oven. I guarantee it will be even better than the practice cake."

"If only I could!" Brindl said, for she truly did wish to spend more time with him. "But I should get back to my birds."

"Tomorrow morning, then? My mother makes the sweetest breakfast rolls you've ever had. Seven bells?"

"It would be a pleasure," Brindl answered happily. She would have to feed the birds earlier than usual, but it would be worth the effort. Finally, she seemed to be making a new friend. "Thank you for helping me."

Tonio smiled, his eyes sparkling again. "It was nothing.

The bakery's not far from the palace. Just follow your nose tomorrow."

"I will," she answered, and turned with a wave.

After she filled her pail and grabbed an additional bag of grain from the stacks inside the building, Brindl followed two white-clad kitchen maids back to the palace. The maids walked quickly, and Brindl struggled to keep up. The grain bag shifted on her hip like a jostling baby while the full pail banged painfully against her knee.

Once inside the palace, Brindl slowed so as not to spill grain on the freshly scrubbed floor, though all the other servants seemed in a panic, rushing through the halls. Judging from snatches of conversation, someone important had arrived unexpectedly and there was to be a formal dinner that night. When Brindl finally arrived on the rooftop, out of breath from all the stairs, she found an invitation tacked to her tower door.

Queen Twenty-two
Requests the presence
of Brindl Tacora
At dinner
This very evening, upon the 7th bell
In the Lilac Room
To celebrate the arrival of
The Queen's Sword,
Jaden Telendor

Do not observe too closely those whom you serve. It is a breach of their privacy. Hold your eyes to the floor whenever possible.

—CH. N. TASCA, *Palace Etiquette*

FOUR

lued in place, Brindl read the invitation several times to be certain it was for her. When she realized what must be done to prepare for such an event, the rest of the day passed in a blur. In addition to her regular duties with the bluejackets, readying her simple uniform to look presentable for dinner with the Queen was no small task. Brindl scrubbed spots out with white powder, hemmed a frayed edge, and sewed a button on the cuff.

Next she washed her hair in a basin and sat in the sun—thank Intiq he'd decided to appear today!—to dry it. She scraped her fingernails clean and filed their jagged edges with volcano stone. Using a hand mirror and a few pins, she attempted to pull her hair into a tidy bun. Finally, she scoured the chamberlain's etiquette book, hoping to glean information she might need as a guest of the Queen. But no. Nothing. Apparently palace servants were not supposed to make eye contact with Royals unless directly addressed, let alone dine with them. *Why in three Gods was I invited anyway?* She had scarcely seen the Queen since her arrival and had certainly never spoken to her. Only twice could she remember catching a glimpse of the monarch swishing down a palace hallway, nearly hidden by her entourage.

Though Brindl left the roof with plenty of time to spare, several false turns later she entered the Lilac Room just as the bells tolled seven. The well-named room had been opulently appointed. Six enormous bay windows looked out to the Sentry Hills, which nearly matched the sublime purple color of the room as dusk settled over them. Each window had been draped with multiple yards of painted silk fabric, and Brindl calculated the price for a single window dressing would have easily fed an Earth Guild family for a year or more.

She turned her attention to the people then, hoping to find a friendly face. Fortunately, it was a small party and she quickly spotted Chey and Tali. *Thank Machué. Friends.* She made a straight path to them, but before she got there a serving maid jingled a small bell, signifying that dinner would begin. Everyone made their way to the long table in the center and stood behind the chair where their name had been indicated by a place setting. Near a far window, Queen Twenty-two seemed in no hurry to end her conversation with Jaden.

Finally, she strode elegantly across the room, her royal white gown almost glowing, as if to match the glass torches lining the walls. The dress was a simple Moon Guild design, though embellished with thousands of tiny seed pearls. She wore little face paint, but her eyes had been outlined to striking effect. Despite her beauty, Brindl thought, there is a glint of cruelty in her gaze.

When the Queen reached the table, the entire company bowed before her. Two finely dressed servants pulled out her chair and she took her place at the head of the table. She nodded to signal the others to sit. Relieved to be seated with Tali and Chey at the farthest end of the table from the Queen, Brindl pressed her hands to her knees, willing herself to be calm. *You have faced dark tunnels miles below the earth on your own. She may be a Queen, but she is still a person, a woman.*

Brindl took a quick look around the table, trying to identify everyone. Princess Xiomara sat to the Queen's left, Jaden to her right. Next came Larus, centurio of the palace guards, and several other men, who, judging by their robes, would be the royal counselors. Zarif was among them, and he nodded briefly in Brindl's direction. A handsome, well-dressed woman sat on the other side of Chey.

A servant came by then and placed a tiny bowl of melon-colored soup in front of each of them. Brindl looked down in consternation at the three different spoons at her place setting. She felt someone nudge her foot and looked across the table to see Chey picking up the smallest spoon. "It is to stir your appetite," he said in a soft tone, "as if I ever need help with it."

Another servant leaned over Brindl's shoulder and poured a sparkling liquid into a tall flute. It looked as if fairies had blown bubbles inside the glass. As Brindl reached for the glass, it clinked loudly against her soup bowl, giving pause to the conversation. Brindl felt her face heat as the Queen's eyes flashed irritation down the table. The monarch smiled thinly, then turned back to Jaden.

Brindl put her glass down without taking a sip. "The Queen is not pleased with my presence," she said quietly to her friends.

"You're being too sensitive. It gets easier, trust me," Chey said.

"I'd prefer to hunt kitchen rats than attend these dinners myself," Tali muttered, "but you won't find a better meal anywhere in the palace, so at least there's that."

Brindl feigned a smile as Tali and Chey turned back to

their discussion of the palace stables and the merits of various breeds of horse. She had little to add to the conversation, so she looked at the woman on Chey's right. "We've not been introduced," she said, forcing another smile. "I'm Brindl, Master of Messages to Princess Xiomara."

"I am Ona, lady's maid to the Queen," the woman replied with a curt nod. Though pretty, her face showed no trace of emotion or warmth. She reminded Brindl of an empty plate. Pristine and flat.

"You must be a member of the royal family, Lady Ona," Brindl continued, determined to be polite even if Ona was not. "You share a resemblance to both the Queen and the princess."

"Cousins," the woman said, then deliberately turned her attention to the other side of the table.

Brindl gave up and listened to her friends speak of horses instead. "Why is Lady Layna not here to attend Princess Xiomara?" she asked Tali during a break in their conversation.

"Layna doesn't feel well," Chey answered, but it was Tali who gave away the truth, muttering, "Again," and rolling her eyes as she took a sip of the bubbly beverage.

"Is she often ill?" Brindl asked.

"No, but Layna hates these dinners. She's afraid of the Queen," Chey whispered.

"She's afraid of her own shadow," Tali corrected.

Though Brindl grinned, she did not blame Layna. She'd happily return to her tower to eat porridge at present. The soup was removed and a beautifully arranged plate of beef and root vegetables was placed in front of her. Brindl took her lead from Chey once more, waiting to pick up her utensils until he did.

At the end of the table Jaden laughed and Brindl watched him for a moment. Compared to the other men around him, he seemed warm and lively, while the Queen's counselors remained stern and arrogant in their speech. Jaden, a tall man even when seated, had assumed his role of Queen's Sword with confidence, despite the shadow he must have felt from his father's dark legacy. Tali, Brindl noticed, could not keep her eyes from trailing over to him. He, too, occasionally glanced down the table at Tali, his searching expression difficult to read.

Lost in thought, Brindl suddenly realized that Jaden was now looking at her expectantly. Chey nudged her under the table. Machué save me, she thought, as all eyes turned to her.

In the end, it was Tali who saved her. "Can you repeat your question, Commander? I don't think Brindl heard you above my exclamations of joy over these fried yucca rounds."

Jaden smiled at Tali, then Brindl. "I asked how our young heroine is adapting to life in Fugaza?"

Brindl looked at him in confusion. Was he talking about *her*?

"Young heroine?" the Queen asked, voicing the same question Brindl had.

"Brindl here was crucial to our victory in the Battle for the Alcazar, Your Majesty," Jaden explained. He turned back to Brindl then. "I never did have a chance to thank you. That's why I asked the Queen to invite you here tonight."

"But I deserve no thanks," Brindl said, trying to keep her voice from quavering under the attention of the entire table. "I handed fiery arrows to a guard on the wall. It was the smallest of tasks. Nothing compared to what *you* did, Commander, nor to what Tali, Chey, and Zarif did," she said, looking around at her friends.

"They were indeed crucial to the battle," Jaden agreed. "Yet it was you who freed them, was it not? They would've remained locked in the dungeon if not for you."

"But I—" Brindl tried to object.

Jaden waved a hand at her. "You also got word to the Diosa at the critical hour. Without her aide, I would not have arrived in time. Without the packhounds and miners, we would have fallen. Some might say we owe the realm to you."

"I am honored you think so," Brindl said, clasping her hands under the table, "but I deserve no praise."

"Nonsense," said the Queen then, raising her glass. "To Brindl, for her service to Tequende," she toasted, her voice festive though her eyes remained cool.

"To Brindl!" repeated the rest of the party, lifting their drinks at once.

Willing her hand not to tremble, Brindl raised her own glass and forced herself to look at everyone. The many faces around the table reflected a newfound recognition of her presence, a respect, she supposed, that had not been there before. Even Lady Ona looked at her differently, her eyes betraying not only surprise but a thin icing of jealousy.

Thankfully, the conversation soon turned back toward broader matters of the realm. "I have empowered Centurio Jessa with the reins of the Alcazar in my absence," Jaden said, in response to one of the counselor's questions.

"Is it wise to leave it unattended, given the recent attack?" Princess Xiomara asked. She had not said much throughout the evening, letting the Queen and Jaden do most of the talking.

"I believe it's more important that I'm visible as the new Queen's Sword rather than squatting at a post that is well prepared to defend itself."

"I meant no offense," Xiomara assured Jaden. "I just wondered about your strategy."

"None taken," he said, wiping his mouth with a napkin.

"I've spent the past months traveling the realm to meet with all my centurios, visiting each outpost in turn, and reviewing our strengths and weaknesses. I'll give you and the Queen a full report tomorrow, but I won't bore your guests tonight."

Their dinner dishes were whisked away then and replaced by individually plated lemon cakes, each one laced with white icing. Brindl smiled, reminded of her meeting with Tonio.

"I met one of the bakers of these amazing cakes just this morning," she said to her friends. "He helped me find the grainery when I was lost on the palace grounds."

"Is he an ancient magician?" Chey asked, stuffing a large bite into his mouth.

"Actually, he's our age," Brindl said, "and very kind. He invited me to the bakery for breakfast tomorrow."

"The young baker sounds as sweet as his cake," Tali said, grinning mischievously. "But tell me, does he look as fine?"

Brindl was saved the embarrassment of a response by raised voices at the end of the table.

"It is quite true," the Queen said to Jaden. "We prepare for the arrival of the regents from both Oest Andoria and New Castille."

"I had heard this rumor, but assumed it was just that: a rumor. Surely you will not treat with these vipers?" asked Jaden.

Centurio Larus answered for her. "If you refer to the

Battle for the Alcazar, Oest Andoria claims innocence. They say they knew nothing of the mercenaries."

A flash of pain crossed Jaden's face. Everybody there knew well that Jaden's father, Commander Telendor, had led those mercenaries himself.

One of the counselors spoke then, his cloying remarks obviously meant to gain favor with the Queen. "The Treaty Talks will usher in a new age of peace and prosperity for Tequende. Our realm will be the envy of the Far World."

"We have the best craftsmen in the lands. We'll fetch a high price for our goods," agreed another, nodding toward the Queen.

The first counselor looked smugly at Jaden. "The regents will be given a grand tour so they might see all we have to offer."

"And expose our weaknesses," Jaden said, pushing back from the table and standing up. "Excellent idea. Then they'll gut Tequende of all its riches as they've done the rest of the Nigh World."

"Sit down," the Queen said, her voice just above a harsh whisper. "Upon the arrival of the regents, you will report directly back to the Alcazar, Commander, lest you offend our guests and ruin my chance for a trade agreement."

"And what of your protection?" Jaden asked quietly, taking his seat as ordered.

"I am well guarded," the Queen answered, indicating Centurio Larus nearby. "You will cordially, and I do mean cordially, greet the regents at the opening ceremonies. Then you will take your leave."

An awkward hush descended over the table. Dessert could not end soon enough for any of them, the lemon cakes suddenly sour on the tongue.

Lady servants will not fraternize with those beyond the palace: develop friendships, if you must, within your own circle of service.

—CH. N. TASCA, *Palace Etiquette*

FIVE

onio had been right. As soon as Brindl stepped out of the palace the next morning, she smelled a sumptuous aroma emanating from a large building nearby, its several chimneys puffing out wispy trails of smoke. The bakery. As the palace bells tolled seven, Tonio stepped through the double doors and smiled widely.

"Brindl! You made it," he said, taking her elbow and pulling her through the entry.

The bakery was spectacular. A dozen people worked in the grand room, displaying an amazing degree of industry and organization. Some chopped ingredients of every color on a wide table that ran down the room's center, while others had their hands deep inside big lumps of dough. Still others stirred giant wooden spoons in huge metal bowls. A tray with enough eggs to feed a giant sat in the middle of the table where the workers reached in and plucked them out in twos and threes.

Blue-painted shelving lined the walls on all sides and gleaming glass containers showed off their contents: flours and sugars, herbs and spices, honeys and oils. Bowls spilling over with fruit sat next to them. High windows above the shelves flooded the room with morning light. Though the bakers bustled about with bowls and trays, somehow without ever bumping into each other, there was a cheerfulness to the room, a warm energy. And the smell! Brindl felt more at ease here in a single minute than she had for the entire evening in the Lilac Room.

She turned to Tonio. "It's a wonder! I never thought a kitchen could be so inviting."

"A bakery is a sweeter place than an ordinary kitchen," Tonio answered, leading her through a chorus of greetings and welcomes.

Such a world of difference from the mines, Brindl thought. No danger, no chill, just a toasty warm room filled with plenty of food. "How nice it must have been to grow up here."

Tonio smiled thinly, and Brindl could see that her

comment made him bristle. She continued to follow him, wondering what she'd said or done wrong, hoping she hadn't just cut her new friendship short.

But Tonio recovered quickly, pointing out some of the stranger ingredients as they traveled through the great room. Some of the items hailed from faraway places whose names she'd never heard before. She bit into a chocolate candy he placed in her palm, delighted when the crunchy outside exploded to cream inside her mouth.

"That's a karnot. I like to hide them inside pastries as a surprise."

"It's delicious!"

"Wait until you try the Saragasso syrup," Tonio said, dipping a small stick into a jar and twirling it until the golden syrup formed a ball.

He handed the stick to Brindl, who popped it into her mouth. The syrup tasted tangy and sweet simultaneously. Then he unhooked the hinge on a jar and pulled out a small pale fruit rolled in sparkling sugar. "A clemente," he said, offering it like a piece of gold. Brindl closed her eyes as the sugar melted on her tongue, giving way to the tart fruit flavor underneath. How could she ever eat plain porridge again?

"Now, this," Tonio said, dipping his hand into yet another jar, "is called a tupelatelo." He opened his hand to show a nut about the size of a Queen's coin, and almost as flat. Though its plain brown husk did not look at all inviting, he offered it to Brindl like a holy piece of salt, blessed by the Diosa herself.

"Go on," he said, placing it into her palm. Brindl took a tentative bite, surprised when a variety of tastes danced inside her mouth, sweet, sour and spicy all at once. It was chewy, too, and took several bites before it finally disintegrated.

"Whatever do you use them for?" she asked.

"Tupelatelos are so rare that we use them only for the most special of delicacies, made once a year on the Queen's birthday."

"And you wasted one on me?"

Tonio laughed. "Your face made it worth it! Like a child on festival day."

Brindl suddenly felt a lump in her throat. Tonio's easy nature reminded her of her brother, Tamind. It caught her off guard, these thoughts of home.

"What is it?" Tonio asked.

"I, well . . ." Brindl hesitated, not wanting to change the mood. "You remind me of my older brother is all, but I don't talk about home."

Tonio gave her a long look. "Not even to your important friends, at least?"

"Never," Brindl answered. "It's easier to pretend I have nothing to miss than to dwell on all that I do."

Tonio nodded. "I understand. Sometimes it's hard to be an only child, but easier than being a second-born, I imagine."

Brindl shrugged. "At least there's one less mouth to feed at home. Tamind could eat his weight in food at each meal."

"I might be able to match him there," Tonio said, gesturing for Brindl to follow him. "I'm sure he'd rather have your company than your portion."

Brindl nodded. "Probably, yes. Our parents are older than most, not all that lively."

"Is that so?" Tonio asked, handing Brindl a small square of bread infused with cinnamon.

"For years and years, no children. Then, two in a row. . . ."

They turned a corner and nearly ran into a woman who could only be Tonio's mother.

"Brindl, meet Mama Rossi," Tonio said, as the two women placed their palms together.

"I'm honored to meet you," Brindl said, dipping her head.

"We're glad you came down from the roof!" Mama Rossi answered, then enveloped Brindl in a warm hug, wrapping her generous arms around Brindl's tiny frame. The unexpectedness of her embrace was a shock, but the larger woman's body felt comforting, too. Mama Rossi pulled back from the hug but did not release her hands, studying Brindl.

Brindl, embarrassed, had no choice but to do the same.

Mama Rossi was, in a word, round. Her hair was piled in a stout bun, her face a full moon. Her body, too, was generous and plump but seemed to suit her just right. Though some of Tonio's good looks peeked through her features, they'd been softened by time and age, and perhaps one too many treats in her welcoming bakery.

"My mother thinks she was born in Fiorenze like my father," Tonio joked. "It is custom there to crush someone you've just met."

"Let me look at you," Mama Rossi said, holding Brindl out farther. "You're all bones, like one of your little birds. You must eat!"

Tonio raised his eyebrows at Brindl. "My mother's answer for everything."

"Hush now, boy. Go get the sweet rolls from the oven. We'll feed her twice before I let her leave!"

Mama Rossi pulled Brindl into a back room, obviously the small quarters she shared with her son. A pretty green cloth, embroidered with flowers, covered a round table. Though none of the four adjoining chairs matched in structure, they were painted the same bright cheerful blue of the shelving in the main kitchen. Paned windows overlooked a large kitchen garden where a few Earth Guilders already bent over the plants in the early morning light.

Mama Rossi shuffled Brindl into a chair and immediately began serving her hot cocoa and twisted rolls fresh from the oven. Inside each warm bite was a taste of honey, sweetberries, and a glazed icing that demanded to be licked from the tips of her fingers rather than go to waste. Tonio returned and sat down beside her. Mama Rossi would sit down in fits and starts before she'd jump up again to fetch something she wanted Brindl to try.

"So Tonio tells me you are from Zipa!"

"Yes, Mistress Rossi."

"Oh, don't call me that formal name, dear. I am Mama Rossi to everyone in the village."

"Have you always lived here in Fugaza, Mama Rossi?" Brindl asked, breaking apart a piece of an enormous flat cake that seemed to be made of a thousand layers. Mama Rossi herself reached over and tore off a generous piece, then dipped it into a honey pot with a warming candle beneath it. Brindl did the same and was surprised when the texture of the cake changed to fluffy instead of flat.

"Oh, yes. A palace kitchen girl my life whole. But my husband, Angelo—Machué protect him—he came from afar," Mama Rossi said, nodding toward the window, as if the sea was just beyond the vegetable patch outside. "Fiorenze."

"He was an artist and scholar there," Tonio added, reaching for his cup of cocoa.

"How then did you two meet?" Brindl asked, turning to Mama Rossi, who handed her another piece of flat cake. Brindl felt like she might burst, but still she took the cake and dipped it in honey.

"Oh, Angelo wanted to see the wide world so he traveled all over. He'd join a ship and work his way across the seas, painting portraits and landscapes for the captains and their rich travelers. We still have his journals and sketches." Mama Rossi paused, crossing her arms over her ample form, and looked dreamily out the window.

She still loves him, Brindl thought.

"Mama, you did not answer Brindl's question yet," Tonio said, placing a hand on her arm.

"Oh, yes, well . . . on one of the voyages he met a wealthy merchant who was on his way here to the Nigh World. The merchant admired Angelo's artwork and suggested Angelo accompany him to Tequende, where art was much in demand. Angelo did so and was soon commissioned to paint a portrait of Queen Twenty. I was a kitchen maid then, and I served him cocoa each day," she said, her voice taking on a wistful quality. "He was so handsome, and I loved his Far World accent."

Tonio added the ending. "He fell for Mama and petitioned to be an Earth Guilder so they could marry."

Brindl heard a certain bitterness underneath Tonio's

words and tried to read his face, but it had set like stone. *How could such a lovely story make Tonio sound this way? He is somewhat of a puzzle.*

"Did he not continue to paint portraits?" Brindl asked.

"Not as an Earth Guilder, no. The art professions belong to those in the Moon Guild. But, he taught me how to make cakes," Mama Rossi said, "and he poured all of his artistry into making them as beautiful as any sculpture or painting."

"We look through his journals still for inspiration," Tonio added, and there it was again, the sharp edge to his voice, like an unexpected cut on a finger.

Mama Rossi glanced at her son and put her hand over his. "We lost Angelo to river fever when Tonio was just eight."

"I've been baking cakes with Mama ever since," Tonio said, squeezing his mother's hand in return.

Brindl watched the two of them as the truth settled upon her. Angelo Rossi had given up much to marry an Earth Guilder and start a new life in Tequende. His homeland. His art. His life. *How much he must have loved Mama Rossi to make such a sacrifice.*

True to her word, Mama Rossi kept Brindl captive until she fed her twice that morning. Once with the sweetbreads, and then an early luncheon, too, a Fiorenzan dish of shell-shaped noodles stuffed with herbs and cheese and spicy meat sauce.

"You must return whenever you like," Mama Rossi said. "It's not right for a girl your age to be alone so much on that roof." She pulled Brindl back into a warm embrace, and Brindl found herself hugging Mama Rossi as if she were her own mother.

How long it's been since I've been fussed over like this.

Tonio walked Brindl to the door of the bakery.

"I'll soon be twice my size if I visit the bakery much," Brindl said, "but I thank you for the best morning I've had since my arrival."

"You're welcome here anytime you tire of talking to birds!"

Never speak to a Royal unless specifically addressed, and then keep your reply deferential and dutiful. When in doubt, "Yes, Your Majesty," or "Yes, Your Highness," will usually suffice.

—Ch. N. Tasca, *Palace Etiquette*

SIX

rindl replayed the whole morning as she swept the aviary. Surely it was the nicest day she'd had since coming to Fugaza. Perhaps others would have loved the Queen's dinner more, but Brindl knew where she belonged, where she felt most comfortable—with people who did the real work of the earth. *Her* people. The bakery had been so warm, so cheerful.

How wonderful it must be to work in such companionship with others.

Just as she finished her task, a loud cough at the aviary door surprised her. She turned to find a man who looked too old to be a messenger frowning at her in irritation. Brindl could see flecks of gray at his temples, and his stout frame had undoubtedly made his trip to the roof difficult.

No matter what I do here I seem to annoy people.

"Brindl of the Zipa Salt Miners?" he asked, his breath heavy from the climb.

"I am she," Brindl answered, keeping her head high. It wasn't her fault the man was winded.

"This is the third time I've tried to deliver a message to you this morning."

Oops. Brindl bit her lip. *Perhaps it is my fault.*

"Princess Xiomara and Commander Jaden await your arrival in the princess's quarters immediately."

Brindl looked down at her uniform, dusty from her work. "I need to wash up first."

"You're late already," the messenger scolded, impatience plainly etched on his face.

"Then five more minutes won't hurt," Brindl answered. No doubt the messenger would apprise the chamberlain of her ill manners.

"Clean yourself, but quickly," he snapped, as if it was his idea in the first place, his eyes lingering on her dirty clothes.

Brindl raced to her quarters and pulled out a spare apron. She brushed the remnants of birdseed and straw from her uniform and slippers, then quickly, with deft fingers, combed her hair and pinned it in place. *What could Xiomara and Jaden want with me? Did I err at dinner last night? Has the chamberlain complained of my service as pigeonkeep?*

The walk down from the roof had never felt longer.

Brindl's legs twitched as the scowling messenger led the way. *Enough!* Brindl scolded herself. *Hold yourself up and be more than they expect. You are Brindl Tacora from the Zipa Mines, daughter of Machué.*

When they finally reached the doors to Xiomara's waiting room, Brindl turned to the messenger and curtsied, a playful smile on her lips. "Many thanks for your fine and gracious company, sir."

The messenger, whose face was already flushed from the journey, turned a deeper shade of red. He opened the doors and for a second Brindl thought he might shove her through them. Instead, he cleared his throat and announced her.

"Brindl Tacora, Your Highness."

The princess and Jaden sat at the far end of the room opposite the chandelier that had fallen not a week ago. Brindl noticed that a new desk now sat closer to the windows, as did several chairs where the two awaited.

"She appears at last," Princess Xiomara said, rising and gesturing toward a large blue chair with a round back.

"I'm sorry for any delay you suffered, Your Highness," Brindl said, bowing and taking her seat. "And you as well, Commander. Please forgive me."

The princess gave Brindl a kind look. "Think no more of it. Jaden and I had much to discuss."

"How are you adjusting to life in Fugaza, Brindl?" asked

Jaden. "I asked the same of you last night, but you weren't given a chance to reply. My apologies."

Brindl sensed a true curiosity behind his words, rather than simple politeness.

"It's a beautiful city," she answered. The truth was she'd seen very little of the royal city. Her pigeonkeep duties had kept her nearly as cooped up as the birds she tended. But it wouldn't do to complain. "Much different than Zipa, my hometown."

"Zipa has an austere loveliness, I've been told," Xiomara said.

"Well, I think so, of course," Brindl agreed. "We are all partial to our homes, I suppose."

"True," Jaden said. "The Alcazar, though a despised place for many, is home to me."

"You were raised there?" Brindl asked.

"More trained than raised, I'd say." Jaden laughed uneasily, then looked away.

He does not wish this conversation to turn toward his father. I should change the subject.

"May I ask why you've summoned me? Is there a problem with my service?" It was against all palace etiquette to question her superiors, but Brindl found she couldn't wait any longer. She was never one for small talk, and the suspense was too much to bear.

"No, no, it is nothing of the sort," Princess Xiomara said.

"In fact," said Jaden, "you have come to our attention for just the opposite reason . . . for your commendable service."

"Your quick observation and action likely saved Lady Layna's life in this very place," Princess Xiomara said, glancing at the restrung chandelier across the room.

"I only happened to be here at the right time, Your Highness." Brindl lowered her eyes. "Any other would have done the same."

"And you are modest to a fault," Xiomara replied. "I see now why you were a favorite with my beloved tutor, Saavedra."

"He taught me many things." Brindl tried to speak without her eyes watering at the unexpected mention of her mentor. "I owe him so very much."

"As do I," agreed Xiomara.

"And as I said last night, Brindl, you were key to our success in the Battle for the Alcazar," Jaden continued.

"It was nothing compared to those who fought." It was not her people's way to boast, and Brindl felt uncomfortable being cast in such light.

"You also handled the dinner with the Queen quite well," Xiomara said, "especially given . . ." The princess paused then, searching for words.

My Earth Guild status? My servant position? Brindl thought wryly, waiting to see how Xiomara would respond.

". . . your short time in service."

Nicely done, Princess. "I'm not sure why then you have summoned me, if you have no concerns."

"We have many concerns, Brindl, but none of them land on your shoulders," Jaden answered, his eyes intent upon hers. "At least not yet. We are worried about the impending visit of the regents from New Castille and Oest Andoria."

Brindl nodded and clasped her hands together on her lap. Her fingers were sweating although they felt ice-cold. She didn't know whether she was expected to answer or simply listen.

Princess Xiomara's eyes met Jaden's and held for an instant. Their hesitation stood in the room like another person.

They're deciding whether they can trust me or not.

"What Jaden is trying to say is that we need your help," the princess finally said. "As you know, my lady's maid has had some difficulty of late."

"The chandelier?" Brindl asked, seeing it fall again in her memory's eye.

"She's not quite recovered from the fright."

"What we'd like you to do," Jaden said, "is act as Princess Xiomara's lady's maid while the regents are here in the palace."

May the Gods have mercy.

"You would attend all the functions that I do . . . Dinners, balls, and receptions, at my side as needed," Xiomara explained.

"But surely Lady Layna will be recovered by the time the regents arrive," Brindl said, trying to keep her face composed as dread wrapped itself around her shoulders. She didn't know the first thing about attending a princess.

As if reading her mind, Jaden asked, "Did you meet the Queen's maid last night? Lady Ona?"

Brindl nodded. How could she forget the chilly woman who wouldn't speak to her?

"Good. Then you'll have also noticed that she listened much and spoke little. This is exactly what we ask of you. Quietly observe all that is going on without others taking notice."

A strained silence followed. Brindl looked down at her hands. She was in no position to defy two of the most powerful people in the realm, but couldn't they see? She was raised in the mines, not the palace. They were asking the wrong person.

"But surely Zarif, Tali, or Chey would be better equipped for such observations," Brindl said, brushing off some imaginary lint from her skirt. "And do they not already have an excuse to be near Princess Xiomara at all times?"

"Yes, they do." Jaden's voice slowed. "And we considered each of them in turn, but they need to focus on their own important tasks."

"And besides, the regents will mind their words and actions in front of a guard or a counselor," the princess said.

"We need someone prim and quiet," Jaden explained, looking carefully at Brindl. "Someone the regents will take for a pretty face, nothing more."

Brindl felt her cheeks grow warm. *A pretty face?* She was flattered to be described as such, but also confused. *So am I to be a spy or a lady?*

The room became quiet, waiting for her response. *Can one say no to a princess?* How simple life on the roof now seemed.

"I will do anything Your Highness commands, of course," Brindl answered, rising from her chair and dropping her eyes to her slippers, where she noticed a scuff of mud. She tucked one foot behind the other, hoping it wouldn't be seen. "But I am no Moon Guilder. Surely that will be a problem with your plan?" As she well knew, all palace attendants and officials, including lady's maids, belonged to the Moon Guild. She hoped the conflict would disqualify her from service.

"Yes, it is a problem," the princess said, tilting her head, "though we concocted a solution while your arrival was delayed."

Brindl felt a twinge of guilt at Xiomara's words. Not only had she made the princess wait for her arrival, but she had left her post on the roof without permission. Still, she couldn't regret her morning with Tonio at the bakery.

"You shall pretend to be betrothed," Jaden said, clasping his hands under his chin. "As such, you can petition for entry to the Moon Guild."

"Betrothed? But how? To whom?"

"To Zarif, of course," Xiomara said. "I trust him completely. He will go along with the pretense if I ask."

Brindl lost her ability to speak and her stomach dropped to her feet. The idea held utter mortification. No no no, her mind rebelled.

"I shall expedite the request myself," the princess added, clapping her hands together. "In a matter of days you shall be a Moon Guilder!"

"But I don't want to be a Moon Guilder," Brindl declared, the words pouring out of her. "Nor do I wish to be betrothed, pretense or not."

"It's not ideal, we realize." Jaden pursed his lips. "But sometimes we must put the realm before our own desires. We need you, Brindl."

"You ask too much!" Brindl insisted, unable to control the distress and volume of her voice. *The Queen owns my service for six years, and now they want my guild, too? Black tunnels!*

Jaden and Xiomara exchanged another look while Brindl dropped back into her chair.

There's something else they're not telling me.

"Do you remember Ory?" Jaden asked.

"Ory?" repeated Brindl, confused by the unexpected question. She'd known Ory since he was nothing more than a tot in the mines. She'd trained him as a firstie and several years beyond that until he was called to serve the Diosa. It was Ory himself who had taken her message to the Diosa during the Battle for the Alcazar. "Yes, of course I remember Ory. He's like a brother to me."

"He came here late last night," Xiomara said.

"Ory did? I don't understand."

"He brought a message from the Diosa. About you."

Brindl's head flew up. The Diosa was the last living oracle of Machué, the spiritual leader of the Earth Guild. What message could she possibly have about Brindl? And for the princess of the realm, no less?

Brindl looked from Xiomara to Jaden. "And the message was?"

Jaden cleared his throat. "When danger nears, let Brindl be your eyes and ears."

A lady's maid is one of the most honored placements in the realm, denoting a Royal's fondness for your company. As such, devote your life to the elegance and gentility required of such an esteemed position.

—Ch. N. Tasca, *Palace Etiquette*

SEVEN

he chamberlain must think me a common country toad," Brindl said, as she walked beside Tonio toward the garden.

"Why? Because you don't dine with seven utensils regularly?" He stopped to look at Brindl. "She's the toad. Don't let her make you feel you're less."

"Toad Chamberlain. That does have a nice ring to it."

"What does Toad Chamberlain make you do all day?" Tonio asked, leading Brindl under a large tree whose long fingers of leaves brushed the cool, thick grass.

"It's ever so Moon Guilder," she said, picking up a few stray sticks. "I must compose my face into a mask of marble, emotionless. My chin must be held at a perfect angle, in a straight line with my toes. I am to hold my posture elegantly and without fidgeting. Even my meals must be made of tiny bites, lest I look hungry."

"Mama would be offended if she saw you eat like that," Tonio said, spreading a blanket under the shade. "Small appetite for food, small appetite for life, she says."

"I have a small appetite for stupidity, and for wasting time, which is all royal life seems to be."

"Ceremonies and formalities, *bleck*!" Tonio said, then mocked a dramatic death as he fell to the woven wool blanket the color of an angry sky.

Brindl nodded and dropped beside him. Then she mimicked the formal tone of the chamberlain: "Now, now, Master Rossi, we do not use the common word for *bleck*. Repeat after me: *royalbleck*! Sit up straight and do stop fidgeting! Your posture is reprehensible, your manners abominable. You grieve me, child!"

Tonio laughed at Brindl's impersonation while he pulled a pastry from the basket. "Mama thought you liked this best."

"How did she know? I don't think I said which one was my favorite last week."

"It was written on your face back when you were allowed to show it." He dipped his hand back into the basket to pull out a small jar of sweet honey. "She said you liked this with it. Apologies that it's not warmed."

Brindl smiled. "I'm sure it will be wonderful either way."

She tore off a bite of the pastry and scooped it in the honey. "I should've brought the book I must memorize to show you," she said, through a delicious mouthful.

"Memorize a whole book?" Tonio asked, then rolled his eyes at the thought.

"*Palace Etiquette*, written by the chamberlain herself," Brindl answered. "It's riveting, as you can imagine. The section on lady's maids is almost as good as the one on lady servants. That one was a gem."

"Sounds awful," Tonio agreed. "But would you rather be back alone on the roof all day?"

Brindl considered the question. "I'm not certain. I have to admit, it is interesting to take part in the princess's affairs, to feel as though I matter here. But it also feels like playing pretend."

"I still can't believe the Queen has allowed an Earth Guilder on the court at last. I'm glad it will be you."

The pastry suddenly turned dry in Brindl's throat, and she swallowed it down with difficulty. She still hadn't told Tonio the truth. She didn't know how. She didn't want to see his eyes when she told him she was betrothed to Zarif, that she would soon be a Moon Guilder. Now when he did discover the truth, he would know she'd intentionally kept it from him. And the worst part was, the "truth" wasn't even the *real* truth. If only she could tell him about the Diosa's message, that she couldn't possibly defy an order from the realm's own spiritual leader. But she'd been sworn to secrecy about that, as well as her pretend betrothal.

Meanwhile, things weren't any less awkward with Zarif. He was as uncomfortable and embarrassed by the arrangement as she was, Brindl could tell. Ever since Xiomara's formal announcement of their engagement two weeks ago, he'd avoided her eyes and barely spoken to her. Every minute in his presence now felt like an hour, and they both tried not to be left alone together.

Brindl knew that evading each other wasn't the answer, but she didn't know what else to do. How easy things used to be between them at the Alcazar! All those evenings in Saavedra's cottage, poring over books and discussing philosophy, history, literature. They'd spent hours talking, laughing, enjoying each moment together. But these days, Zarif seemed much more comfortable in the company of Princess Xiomara herself, their easy rapport pinching Brindl with jealousy. She tried to push the feeling aside when it came—she knew it was unreasonable—but still it remained, like rock salt on the tongue.

Her old friendship with Zarif was gone now, and soon, she feared, she would lose Tonio, too. What would the baker's son think of her when she stood before him in the clothes of a Moon Guilder? Xiomara's handmaidens had been delighted to make her into a Moon Guilder earlier that morning. But when Brindl looked at herself in the mirror, she felt as if she'd been slapped. All she could see was a traitor before her, not the beautiful white gown nor the lovely flowers woven in her hair. She'd changed her clothes and pulled the flowers out before coming to see Tonio, but soon her new appearance would not be so easy to set aside.

"Hello, have your thoughts flown to the roof with your birds?" Tonio asked.

"Sorry, I was just thinking about all I should be doing." Brindl felt her insides turn from the fib.

Tonio lay back with his hands under his head. "I feel like we're hiding under a giant's green wig." The tree's leaves cascaded around them, whispering slightly in the breeze. When he sat up and reached for another piece of bread, Brindl could smell the bakery on him, a touch of cinnamon, sweet cream, and flour.

"I should get back to my birds," Brindl said, "though I don't want to go."

"You'd think now that you're almost a lady's maid, they'd relieve you of your pigeonkeep duties."

"Oh, but I've begged them to let me stay on. I'd miss the birds too much, and besides, I'm grateful to return to my tower at night after all the daily lessons."

Tonio packed up the basket while Brindl shook the leaves out of the blanket. As they walked to the bakery, two young men about Tonio's age struggled to drag a load of heavy marble blocks past them to the palace garden. The men nearly looked like sculptures themselves, their muscles chiseled by their heavy labors and covered with the white dust of the pearlstone. Their dark hair was worn in the traditional, plain cut of Earth Guilders, though one had a mop of curls.

"It's Tonio," the one with curly hair called out, "and his new girl!"

The other young man elbowed his friend and whistled.

Brindl's face warmed as she bit back a smile.

Tonio flashed her a sheepish look, then led her over to the men and introduced them: Spider and Flea of the Quarry. When their palms parted after the traditional greeting, a chalky white film remained on Brindl's hand. Brindl instantly liked the two of them, who reminded her of the rough-and-tumble salter boys back home: hardworking and solid, their faces open and ready for mischief. But these quarrymen were much bigger than salters and carried themselves with more authority. *Perhaps because they're not forced to scurry below the earth like ants all day.*

"How is it two strong quarrymen are named after insects?" Brindl asked.

"No one in the quarry uses their godnames."

"We're known by our moves in the Fray, like Spider here. He's all legs."

Brindl wasn't sure what they meant, but before she could ask more questions, the two went back to their teasing.

"Brindl, is it? You must be new here," the one called Flea

said. "Tonio always swipes the new girls before they've seen all their options." He flexed an arm muscle when he said it, a wide grin splashed over his face.

Brindl smiled. *Just like home.*

"How can we ever compete with Mamma Rossi's sweet-breads and Tonio's dreamy, Fiorenzan eyes?" Spider said in a mocking tone, his hand to his forehead as if swooning.

"Enough already." Tonio pushed Flea, who took a step backward good-naturedly, though he was clearly as solid as the stone he stood beside.

Spider threw up his hands and laughed. "Fine! Fine. We'll not fight you for her."

"Speaking of fights, there's a good one coming up," Flea said, moving the conversation in a different direction. "Right, Spider?"

"Best one ever," Spider agreed.

"I'll look forward to it," Tonio said. "Full Moon Fray?"

Flea nodded. "Bring your Brindl to it. I bet she's seen nothing like it in Zipa."

After their good-byes, Brindl and Tonio resumed their walk.

"So what exactly is a Full Moon Fray?" Brindl asked, as they reached the bakery doors.

"I have to keep some secrets," Tonio said, with a playful look on his face, "so you'll come back again."

"Then so I shall." Brindl waved good-bye, determined to swallow her worries for the rest of the day.

The mountain breeze slipped into Brindl's collar and sent a chill down her spine. The Sun God was making his descent behind the Sentry Hills, providing a pink cast upon the terrace. After Brindl had left Tonio and tended the birds, she had received a summons from Xiomara, who wished to meet with her retinue to discuss the upcoming Treaty Talks. Brindl shivered again and looked longingly to where the princess stood on the far side of the terrace. *I could warm my bones in that patch of sun.*

The sun lit up Xiomara's ivory gown and she seemed to glow in the light. The pearlstone terrace jutted off the palace like the wing of a bird, the great Magda River rushing below it. Filled to bursting with exotic and native plants, the terrace was a cacophony of color and smell. Soft pink starbursts spilled out of a container in one corner, while a tall, grass-like plant waved purple cups from another. Bright orange trumpet-shaped blossoms twisted through the white carved posts where several gardeners bent over their work, pruning, planting, and sweeping. One of them looked vaguely familiar, but Zarif spoke then, and Brindl turned her attention back to the assembled party.

Zarif, Jaden, Tali, and Chey all sat around her on curved

benches that circled a mosaic fountain, which gurgled quietly. Only the princess remained standing.

"The Andorian regent, Paulin of the famous Matalin family of warriors, will be our most difficult guest in my estimation," Zarif told the princess, who nodded as she paced between two fruit trees, her arms crossed over her bodice and one hand perched by her mouth.

"Why will he be more difficult than the Castillian?" Jaden asked, tapping his fingers on the bench. His handsome face looked chiseled into two colors: worry and anger. Jaden had made no bones about his disapproval of the Queen's Treaty Talks and Brindl could not disagree.

"Paulin is easily offended, a bit short of temper," Zarif replied.

"And the Castillian?" Xiomara asked, pausing near Zarif's bench as she paced.

"Lord Yonda is much older, calmer, and staid in his approach. Our only difficulty will be satisfying his enormous appetite. We'd best lay in plenty of meats and sweets for him."

"The royal bakery and their amazing cakes should be a diversion for him at least," Tali said, grinning. "Right, Brindl?"

Brindl tried to keep her face neutral, as her copy of *Palace Etiquette* had instructed. Never give away your feelings, she reminded herself, as a flash of movement caught her eye.

Danger! the voice inside her warned.

"Watch out!" she yelled, as one of the gardeners pulled out a knife and sent it flying in a terrible arc toward the princess.

Tali leapt instantly, pushing Xiomara to the marble floor. The knife embedded itself in Tali's shoulder and she fell with a groan of pain.

"Chey! Before he escapes!" yelled Jaden, hurtling over the bench to shield Tali and Xiomara, his eyes scanning in all directions for other sources of danger. "Take him alive!"

Chey raced across the terrace, drawing the hammer from his belt.

Zarif fumbled for his crutches, his eyes never leaving the princess, who tried to rise. "Stay down!" he called.

Chey rushed the attacker and pinned him to the balcony, the hammer a menace above his head. "Don't move!" Chey growled, gripping the man by the front of his tunic.

Jaden barked out a command. "Who sent you? Answer us or die!"

Brindl let the air out of her lungs and realized she had been holding her breath since the knife flew.

The man wrenched himself free from Chey's grip. "I'll die, then. But not by your hand," he yelled, throwing himself over the balcony to the raging river below.

Palace servants should never be more than ten minutes from their post even during their hours of leisure and privacy. At any time they may be pressed into service and must be available in case of emergency or requirement.

—CH. N. TASCA, *Palace Etiquette*

EIGHT

L ater that day, Brindl watched Jaden's face change from commander to friend as he closed the door and crossed the sitting room to Xiomara. He reached her in a few decisive strides and gathered her hands in his own.

"How do I find you, Princess?"

"Well enough. And how is Tali?"

"Stitched up and recovering. She says it's a mere scratch compared to her wounds at the Alcazar," he said, glancing over at Chey with a nod.

"That's a relief," Zarif answered, rising from his seat across from Brindl.

"And what did you tell the doctor?" Xiomara asked Jaden, releasing his hands and walking over to her preferred seat, a simple chair near the window.

"A training accident," Jaden answered.

"Believable," Chey offered from his post near the garden door.

"What will you say of the gardener?" Brindl asked, unable to control her curiosity any longer.

"That he committed suicide out of homesickness," Zarif answered, without looking at her.

"It's imperative this secret never leave the room." Princess Xiomara made brief eye contact with each of them in turn. "Otherwise the Queen will use it as an excuse to keep me hidden during the regents' visit. She knows I share Jaden's concerns about the Treaty Talks."

"Have we learned anything of use about the gardener?" Chey asked.

"Little," Jaden said, with a heavy sigh. "Initial reports indicate that he was from the Castillian colony of Las Flores, a tropical island in the Azuria Sea. He was a recent gift from Castille for Princess Xiomara's sixteenth birthday. He was nearly mute with other staff and kept himself isolated."

"Then the suicide story is believable enough," Zarif said, "though it is a compelling detail that he was a gift for Xiomara's sixteenth birthday. . . . Symbolic of her rise to power now that she is officially Queen-in-Waiting."

"So you think he was intentionally sent to kill me?" Xiomara asked Zarif, her voice steady, though she gripped the arms of her chair tightly. "Why?"

"The first question is who installed him. Then we can determine why," Jaden said.

"The obvious answer points to the Castillians," Zarif answered, but his eyes looked to the ceiling, weighing other options. "Of course, that would be just what the Andorians would like us to believe if they did it."

"Exactly," Jaden stated.

"So we do not know which kingdom wants me dead," Princess Xiomara said, reaching for a lace handkerchief on a side table. Brindl noticed that the princess's fingers trembled slightly as she picked up the dainty embroidered fabric.

"It could be either," Zarif said, his usually neutral face betraying worry for once.

"Or both," Brindl finished, surprising everyone with her words.

"You mean that the two kingdoms might be working as one? It seems unimaginable, given their tumultuous history as enemies," Zarif said.

"At this point," Chey asked, "should we rule out any theory?"

"Absolutely not," Jaden said.

"Then we should also consider," Brindl glanced at the princess before she finished, "that it could be someone inside Tequende as well."

"True," Jaden answered, nodding.

The princess looked pale and immovable as pearlstone. "You called out, Brindl, before any of us knew what was happening. Your warning may well have saved my life. What did you see that we didn't?"

Brindl replayed the memory in her head. "I think I recognized the gardener. He looked like the same man I saw cleaning the sconces outside this room before the chandelier fell."

"Are you certain, Brindl?" Zarif asked, his gaze pointed, almost accusatory. "I thought you said you didn't see that man's face? I asked the chamberlain, and she insisted that no one had been assigned to clean the sconces that day."

All eyes were on Brindl now. The attention felt like the sun in her face, glaring hot.

Brindl considered her answer. Was she certain? Yes, but only because her inner voice had been so insistent. "No," she lied, unable to admit how she knew, lest they think her half-mad.

"But the princess could have died that day as well," said Chey, glancing at Xiomara. "It seems more than coincidence, does it not?"

Brindl shifted in her chair.

"You came!" Tonio said, offering Brindl a hand up the first rocky patches of the path. His hair looked darker without the usual dusting of flour, and his bright eyes flickered in the fading light.

"Did you think I wouldn't?" she asked. It had been a whirlwind of a week since Brindl had last seen him. The palace remained in the dark concerning the assassination attempt on Xiomara, but each day the inner circle burned with intensity because of the secret. Everyone was on edge, ferreting out real and imagined danger. If that wasn't enough, the chamberlain had been ruthless with her lessons. Thank the Gods Brindl had received Tonio's invitation. It was a relief to have one thing to look forward to in her week.

"I wasn't sure you could get away with the regents arriving so soon."

"It has been relentless, to be sure," Brindl answered, wishing she could tell him more. In some ways, Tonio seemed as safe as a brother. Still, it would not be her lips to betray Xiomara's trust.

"Mama has been asking about you. She worries that you're overworked and not getting enough to eat."

"Doesn't she think that of everyone?"

"True." Tonio grinned and pulled Brindl to the edge of the path. The track to the other side of the mountain switched back and forth in steep, jagged stripes. A mule cart sounded below them, the loud bells around the animals' necks giving fair warning to provide a wide berth.

"Tonio!" a young man called from the back of the cart. "Hop on!"

"We can't stop the mules, so make a jump for it!" another boy said, laughing.

Brindl and Tonio skipped up to the cart, where half a dozen other young people already sat on stacks of hay.

"Won't we be too much for the poor animals?" Brindl asked.

"Oh no, it's a whole team of beasts. And they're used to heavy pearlstone. Go on, jump in!"

Brindl took a running leap and hoisted herself into the cart, followed by Tonio, while the others cheered them on. After Tonio made the introductions, he pulled the cloth bag off his shoulder and produced sweet treats courtesy of Mama Rossi.

He handed Brindl a small, buttery biscuit. As soon as she bit into it, the flavors melted in her mouth like a sun-drop on the tongue. A young groundsman passed around a bottle of fruitshine, which made Brindl's eyes water with a single swallow and produced a warmth in her stomach that expanded all the way to her fingers and toes.

As the group enjoyed their small feast, two young men began playing a spritely tune on their hand instruments, a song Brindl recognized from festival days in Zipa. The cart continued back and forth up the mountain, allowing views of the palace more beautiful than ever, cast in the amber light of Intiq going to bed. Brindl let her worries slip away and joined in the chorus of the song, content to be exactly where she was.

If time should find you far from here,
Sweet memories may reappear,
Small gifts from days long turned to dust,
But live inside each one of us.

Soon after, they arrived on the other side of the mountain. Brindl hopped down from the cart and stood in wonderment.

So this is Quarry Town.

Built on the edge of the pearlstone quarry itself, the buildings hung over the vast crater like bird nests, one side looking out over the sheer quarry cliff, the other facing the village street and mountains beyond. Though quite narrow, the stacked homes towered several stories high, each one painted its own bold hue: burnt oranges, amber, teals and greens, now muted in the waning light. Brindl tried to imagine the vast views their inhabitants must have of the raw and jagged beauty outside their windows.

How far they must be able to see, like raptors perched high above the world.

"Good eve," strangers greeted her as they passed. "A perfect night for the Fray."

A growing throng of villagers poured out of the unique dwellings, all moving toward the giant crater. The Moon Goddess Elia appeared dimly in the sky, preparing to shed her light on the colorful, peculiar village as her brother set in the west. Brindl found it hard to look away from the scene, as if she'd taken a ship over the wide sea to another land, rather than a mule cart to the other side of a mountain.

"Look at the pearlstone paths leading to the quarry," Tonio said, turning around to Brindl. "See how they reflect each color of the sunset?"

"It's beautiful," she answered. "Almost like a painting that can change on its own."

"Sculptures made of pearlstone are renowned throughout the Far and Nigh Worlds for that very reason," Tonio said, his face relaxed and content.

He's happier here than in the bakery, Brindl realized. Perhaps it was merely due to the day off, but Brindl sensed something deeper. Wistful even.

Down, down they went along a path lit with oil torches, spitting and smoking, into the great quarry crater. When they neared the bottom, Brindl understood why the events were held here. A large flat, square area lay in the center, lit by dozens of torch poles. All around them, the walls of the quarry had been carved into receding layers, creating the perfect seating for the large, raucous audience. It reminded Brindl of one of Tonio's amazing cake designs with its tiers.

Tonio spread the same soft blanket that he'd used for their picnics onto a pearlstone ledge, sharing it with another couple from the cart. Their legs dangled off the edge, almost as if they had climbed the tall limb of a tree.

"Why does the Fray not take place during the day?" Brindl asked Tonio.

"There are no days off in the quarry."

"Much like Zipa, then," Brindl answered, "where the salt comes first. Here the pearlstone."

"And bread is made each day as well, though it is far easier to lift," Tonio joked.

Brindl had never been in one place with so many people, and all of them Earth Guilders, too. How hardworking and earnest they appeared. Brindl was proud to be a part of these people, for they truly made the realm move forward with their faces marred by dust and dirt, their hands a landscape of calluses. Quarry women, with hair covered by colorful fabrics, weaved through the crowd collecting donations in large baskets. When one passed under their feet, Tonio stopped her and offered several coins as well as a loaf of Mama Rossi's bread.

"This is how Quarry Town takes care of its sick and elderly. People give all they can each month at the Fray," he said, pointing to an area where Brindl now noticed a large stash of corn, coffee, yucca, and an assortment of salted meats and fish.

"They know how to take care of one another here," Brindl said.

A quartet of musicians walked through the crowd and across the arena in random patterns, filling the pit with traditional Tequendian folk music. The instruments themselves—two handheld string guitars, a sea horn, and a gourd filled with pebbles and grains—were painted in bright colors, much like the houses of the village. A skinny dog with ears too large for its face followed the band wherever they went, a hollowed-out gourd strapped to his side. As the band moved through the crowd, the people's faces lit up around them. When they ventured closer, Brindl watched people call the pup over to give it a scratch behind the ears and drop a few coins in the gourd.

Before long, an old man walked to the center of the square. The crowd hushed as the music stopped. Even though he was quite elderly, the man still looked enormous compared to the miners back home. Twice their size easily, thought Brindl, and well past his sixtieth harvest.

The old man held up his hands and began. "As always, there will be two matches tonight. Each match has two parts. The first will last fifteen minutes. The second, if it happens, for five. Honor over strength."

"Honor over strength!" the entire crowd answered, and their words seemed to echo out of the canyon of rock.

"Honor rules demand a clean fight," continued the old

man. "Wins shall be determined by knockout, submission, or fan vote. First match, Fury versus the Goat!"

The crowd roared again as the old man walked off the arena grounds.

Tonio leaned toward Brindl. "The men who fight are enormous, you'll see."

"Men? No women?"

"Women would not make good fighters, I think," Tonio answered.

Tali would certainly argue against that point! Brindl thought, but she held her tongue. "So does fan vote mean the audience can decide a fight?" she asked.

Tonio nodded. "Hopefully you'll get to witness one; it's something to see!"

A horn sounded and two men strode out of the shadows into the flickering light of the quarry floor. They were of different sizes, one noticeably bigger than the other, though the shorter, balder man looked wide as a cart. The bigger one, Fury, as Tonio called him, entered the arena with a terrible scowl on his face. Then he lifted his chin, cupped his hands around his mouth, and gave a haunting howl. The crowd, fired up with his encouragement, suddenly leapt to their feet, pumping their arms in the air and howling back. Fury obviously knew how to work a crowd into a frenzy.

Fury gave one last howl, then turned to his opponent.

The shorter, wider fighter, known as the Goat, wasted no time and charged the bigger man as soon as they faced each other. Unlike Fury, the Goat never acknowledged the crowd, his face a mask of singular determination. A crisp, almost elegant punch sliced into Fury's face, cracking the confidence in it.

The Goat followed each punch with another, so sharp and with such power that Fury was pushed a step at a time toward the ring of torches. Fury tried to swing back, but the Goat easily dodged him, then ended the match with one final blow of his fist. Fury fell in a heap, his feet at an odd angle to the rest of his body. He did not rise for many seconds and the crowd waited breathlessly. Brindl wondered if he might be dead, but just then he tossed his head from side to side and moaned. The crowd erupted in cheers and the Goat lifted both his hands in victory, his chin high and eyes bright.

"Goat!"

"Goat!"

"Goat!"

The crowd screamed his name, but the fighter merely nodded and walked out of the light. Several men helped Fury to his feet and ushered him off the arena floor, his head hung in shame or pain. Perhaps both, thought Brindl.

The musicians and their dog took center stage again and people hopped to their feet to twirl on their ledges, looking like dolls dancing to the lively music. Tonio offered Brindl a hand and they joined the rest, laughing merrily as they spun around. Such a contrast to the brutality of the fights! Brindl enjoyed herself, swept up by the gaiety of the music, the troubles of the last week forgotten.

When it was time for the second fight to begin, both fighters stalked onto the arena like they owned it, ready for anything. There was no yelling this time, no baiting the crowd, just a very intense stare down between the two men. It seemed to Brindl that hatred sparked there, live as fire. Better matched in size and weight, one had painted his hair white to differentiate himself.

"Nobody likes the Warrior," Tonio whispered to Brindl, pointing at the one with white hair. "They say he cheats."

Brindl wondered but did not ask how cheating occurred in a brutal sport that looked like nothing was fair.

"What's the other fighter's name?" Brindl asked.

"Axe."

"Sounds ominous," she said, thinking about the mothers of these giant men. How did they feel about their sons giving up their godnames to be called things like Fury and Axe?

As soon as the horn sounded, the Warrior rammed Axe in the gut like a crazed animal, but Axe still managed to pull him to the ground. They exchanged several punches as they grappled before they stood once more, circling. Brindl could not take her eyes off the match, both horrified and fascinated by it. The fight seemed so raw, so personal. Though the crowd was noisy, Brindl could still hear every blow land, every grunt of pain when a punch connected, the guttural growls, like cornered dogs. Tonio explained to her that kicking, punching, and wrestling were all fair options, but the fighters were not to go beyond the circle of torches, lest they hit the pearlstone.

The Warrior threw Axe back down to the ground, then wrapped himself around him, braiding his legs and arms and locking him in place. The two men became a terrible insect monster scrabbling around the dusty floor of the arena.

"Axe him! Axe him! Axe!" Tonio shouted. Other members of the audience picked up his chant.

"Axe him!"

"Axe him!"

"Axe!"

Brindl found that she was breathing into her hands, hoping the fight would soon be over. Then, the two men were on their feet once more. Axe jabbed the Warrior several times, decisively taking control of the match, and was about to finish him off with a knee jab to the chin, when the Warrior grabbed a stray piece of stone and pounded it into Axe's eye.

Axe reeled away, moaning and covering his face with his hands. The crowd gasped as the Warrior took advantage of his sudden weakness to throw Axe down and choke him with his knee. Axe tapped the ground twice with his left hand to signal surrender, but the Warrior did not let go until Axe lost consciousness.

The crowd stood and booed wildly, including Tonio and Brindl. Then they began to chant the name of the loser, Axe, again and again until Axe came to. The old man raised Axe's hands over his head and declared him the winner.

"Honor over strength!" the old man proclaimed, and the crowd repeated his words with enthusiasm. Brindl added her voice to the chorus, finally understanding what just happened. The people had decided that the loser deserved to win more than the man who won by false moves.

"Honor over strength!" she proclaimed, surprised by how much she liked the event after all.

A lady's maid must never engage in idle chatter with palace servants. If you are in want of conversation, choose another lady's maid, for she will provide more pleasant and suitable company.

—CH. N. TASCA, *Palace Etiquette*

NINE

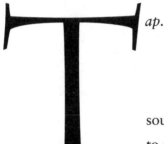 *ap.*

Tap.

Tap.

In bed, Brindl turned against the sound, throwing an arm over her ear to muffle it. Again, she heard it.

Tap.

Tap.

Tap.

She pressed her palms into her eyes, groaned, and reached for the robe to cover her nightdress. *Could it be morning already? Impossible.* Brindl stumbled toward the heavy wooden door, cracking her toe on the only chair in the room. "Black tunnels!" she swore under her breath and finally managed to unlatch the door. She found a young girl standing there.

"I am Lili," the little girl said, offering her left palm to Brindl. The child's smile seemed to steal most of her face. Brindl placed her palm on the girl's and bowed.

"How can I help you this early morning, Lili?"

"It's not so early now!" Lili answered, dipping her head to one side. "Why, even the horses are fed and the stalls cleaned already."

"I see," Brindl said, though she didn't. Nonetheless, she opened the door and motioned the girl inside.

"I'm here to help," Lili said, looking around Brindl's tower room.

"Help with what, exactly?" Brindl walked toward the stove to prepare a strong coffee to clear her head of cobwebs.

"With the birds, of course," Lili said, plucking the kettle from the counter and filling it with water. The girl obviously knew how to make herself useful. "You'll be too busy with the regents, right?"

It was true. The regents were expected to arrive that very afternoon. Brindl nodded, hoping her nerves didn't show on her face.

"At least you got to go to the Fray last night with your sweetboy." Lili put the kettle on top of the burner and grabbed the broom from the corner.

"Tonio? He's not my sweetboy, just a friend," Brindl

answered firmly, wondering what the girl had heard or seen. She was supposed to be betrothed to Zarif, after all. At least that's what everyone in the palace was to believe.

"He's not as sweet as a quarryman, I think," Lili said, sweeping around the edges of the small kitchen area.

"Quarrymen sweet? That's not exactly how I'd describe them," Brindl replied, remembering the huge fighters from last night.

"But you're wrong, you know." Lili stopped her work to look up at Brindl like a love-struck puppy. "They're sweet like honey to the gals they love."

"Lili, how old are you? Aren't you a little young to be thinking of boys?"

"I'm ten harvests already."

"Practically all grown up, then." Brindl winked, but the girl seemed unaware that she was being teased.

"That's what I tell my older sister. 'Course I'm second-born, so I'll have to be a servant to the realm until I'm twenty-one. But then"—Lili paused dramatically—"then I can find me a quarryboy."

Brindl smiled. The girl obviously didn't consider the option of becoming a soldier in the Second Guard, just as she herself had not. And why should Lili? She'd probably never even held a sword or bow in her hand.

"Do you go often to the Fray?" Brindl asked, grabbing

the boiling pot with a dishtowel and pouring it over the ground coffee beans.

"Every chance I get!" Lili said, pounding the corner with the broom, trying to release the stubborn cobweb stuck there. "It's the most exciting thing ever all year."

"I liked it more than I thought I would," Brindl admitted, pouring a splash of milk into her cup. She gestured toward Lili to ask if she wanted some. The girl smiled and nodded, so Brindl grabbed her an extra cup and poured plenty of milk in it.

"Just wait until the next one! It will be even better!"

"Really? How do you know?" Brindl asked, cutting two slices of cornbread and putting them on a plate.

"Because it's Moth versus Pretty Boy!"

"I don't know the fighters," Brindl admitted, sitting down and motioning for Lili to join her. The girl leaned the broom against the corner and sat down.

"Well, my uncle is Moth. He's the best fighter there is. Never been beat, not once."

"Undefeated?"

"He always wins, ayup."

"Did you grow up in Quarry Town then?"

"Oh, no. I grew up right here in the palace stables," Lili said, her finger pointing out the window toward the south where they were located.

"So how did a quarryman become your uncle?"

"That's easy. My aunt, she married him. I'm going to marry a quarryman, too, and live out in Quarry Town someday."

"You mentioned that," Brindl said.

Lili talked animatedly about many different topics, none of them readily connected except by the fact that she wanted to see it, try it, or eat it. Brindl, completely charmed by the little girl, found herself wanting to reach over and wipe the stray hair out of her big brown eyes. It was such a small thing, but having someone join her for breakfast made her realize exactly how lonely she'd been in the tower.

After they ate, Brindl showed Lili her routine of taking care of the birds, adding seed, freshening the water, and alternating which cages to clean. Lili chattered while they worked, mostly about Quarry Town.

"What do the women in Quarry Town do?" Brindl asked. "They can't possibly carry pearlstone, can they? It's so heavy."

Lili waved her hand at such a silly notion. "No, 'course not, but they do other things and help take care of all those workers."

"Those men must have appetites to match their size."

"Exactly. Lots of women make meals and deliver them to the quarry by alpaca," Lili said, scooping up seed for the birds.

"So the women run the kitchens?" Brindl asked.

"Ayup. And others run transportation to the quarry or give grades to the stone."

"Grades? You mean they judge it on how good it is for color or quality?" Brindl thought of the salt miners at home, who did much the same thing.

"I guess so," Lili said, shrugging.

Brindl pulled Pip out of the smallest cage, the one she saved for last, and showed Lili how to scratch the back of the bluejacket's head. The bird cooed softly in Brindl's palms and turned his head sideways, the tiny black eye blinking slowly. Lili looked up at Brindl and cupped her hands. Brindl nodded and gently put the baby in her sturdy fingers. Lili pulled the bird close to her face, and he pecked at her lips lightly.

"What do I do if there's a message?" Lili asked, worry crossing her pretty brown face for the first time since she arrived.

"Oh, yes," Brindl said, opening the cage while Lili carefully put Pip back inside. "There have been very few lately, but send for me if one arrives."

"Good! I wouldn't know how to take it off their leg or even read it," Lili said.

Of course the girl can't read, Brindl thought with a small twinge. Perhaps she could figure out a way to change that for Lili as Saavedra and Zarif had for her.

"Will you be staying in the tower with me during the regents' visit?" Brindl asked, locking the cage without having to look at it.

"Oh, no. I'll go back to the stables each night to sleep. I'd miss my mama and sisters too much!"

"Of course you would, you should be with your family," Brindl said, though she felt a snag at her heart. How nice it would have been to share her tower with this little ray of sunshine!

Brindl pinched her pinky behind her back, trying to focus and calm her nerves. She stood near the wall several steps back from the officials, behind and to the right of the princess, a spot created for watching everything. Jaden had seen to that. All was ready for the regents, who were being presented formally to the court in a matter of minutes. Their entourages had arrived from both neighboring kingdoms within hours of one another, and they'd been given time to rest and prepare for the formal ceremony. Dozens of servants had been reassigned to both parties. Brindl had heard them complaining quietly as she went about her tasks. When it was finally time, she'd been ushered into the Queen's throne room. Never had she seen such a chamber as this, even compared to the dozens of others in the palace.

The room was really two in one. The first encompassed

the entryway, with glass doors that shattered light like a million gemstones on the floor. A large fountain, made of pearlstone of course, cascaded a liquid that appeared to be something finer than water, both brighter and clearer. Large topiary bushes sat in each corner of the room, pruned into sharp edges, almost threatening with their points. A chandelier of a thousand candles lit the room, their bright flickering light casting golden shadows behind each servant and attendant. Two staircases split around the great fountain and curved to the top where the second room stood overlooking the first.

The upper room was an even grander portrait of power and authority. Heavy plum drapes framed a dozen windows, and carpets softened the floor in scrolling patterns. Three equally spaced sconces lit the wall behind Queen Twenty-two's throne, where portraits of the previous twenty-one Queens stared down from gilded frames.

Brindl watched as Lady Ona approached her. "Prepared for pomp and boredom?" Ona asked, leaning over to whisper in Brindl's ear.

Brindl smiled thinly. "Yes, I think so."

"I hear you've shed your Earth Guild origins to become a lady," Ona said, a smirk across her lips.

"I've no shame in my origins," Brindl whispered, trying to keep the anger out of her voice.

"Betrothed to Zarif Baz Hasan, no less," Ona continued, her voice pleasant though her eyes revealed nothing but condescension. "A fine catch for a miner's daughter."

Brindl pinched her pinky even harder and said nothing.

"Much improved," Ona added, as if in satisfaction. "Nearly unrecognizable."

"What is?"

"You. Almost as if you were born a Moon Guilder. Almost." The extra word sliced off any compliment hidden behind it. Brindl wasn't sure if she should respond. It was true enough, though. When she'd peered into the looking glass in Xiomara's dressing room she had barely recognized herself—her hair done elegantly, the white full-length gown draped from her shoulders.

A tap of the drum alerted them to the arrival of the regents. *At least Lady Ona will shut up now.*

All one hundred Second Guard palace soldiers stood in formation from the entry doors below all the way up the staircases to the foot of the Queen's throne. The message was plain: we are well prepared to defend ourselves and the realm. How fine they looked in the bright blue of Tequende, with white sashes for the ceremony. Tali and Chey stood along the steps while Jaden posted himself next to the Queen's throne, impressive with his medals and ribbons adorning his finest uniform.

Princess Xiomara sat to the right of the throne, one step down. Zarif perched behind her left shoulder as if he'd always been there. Brindl noticed Tali's eyes cut to the Queen and Jaden.

The regent from New Castille plodded up the stairs, winded by the time he reached the top. He hesitated before proceeding to the Queen, wiping his wide brow with a kerchief and removing his soft butter-colored gloves. No wonder he perspires so, Brindl thought. He wears layers as if he traveled to a mountain peak instead of a palace. The garments themselves had been created with the finest materials, velvets and satins, and embroidered with golden threads. His pants gathered below his knees, and his lower legs were clad in hosiery and short leather boots with pointed toes. A black hat with a wide, floppy brim embellished with a dark purple feather had been tucked under his arm. He was an enormously fat man, the largest Brindl had ever seen. The effect of his many layers of clothing and girth seemed to demand attention, which he appeared to relish.

As he approached the Queen, he bowed elegantly, his hat somersaulting in his outstretched arm, one foot pointed, the other bent deeply. The Queen rose from her throne, stepped down the tiered dais, and offered her left palm, face up. He placed his palm on hers, aware of the customs of the realm.

"Welcome to Tequende," Queen Twenty-two said,

bowing her head slightly. Her elegant Moon Guilder gown, in shades of white, cream, and vanilla, spilled to the floor. The regent from Castille looked like an overdone pudding in comparison while the Tequendian Queen could pass for a goddess.

"Lord Yonda, emissary from Castille, at your service, my Queen." He bowed once more, lower this time, his head nearly touching his knee.

"May Intiq bless your days and Elia your nights during your stay in Tequende," the Queen said.

"Neither Far nor Nigh Worlds can compete with the renown of Tequende's art, music, and food."

"Thank you, Lord Yonda," the Queen said, taking his hand and leading him to a place on the dais. "I look forward to our visit."

"Not half as much as I do," he said, kissing the top of her hand. The Queen moved back in front of the throne to receive the Andorian regent, who next appeared at the top of the stairs.

He was quite young for such a lofty position and cut an elegant figure with his black hair and eyes. He wore a bloodred military uniform with detailed embroidery along the cuffs and edges. A silver cape snapped around his neck and shimmered in the candlelight. He bowed.

"Queen Twenty-two of Tequende, may I present you with

a token of peace brought to you from my lady, the Queen of Andoria." He handed her a small box, intricately carved and painted red with gilded latches. The Queen did not open the box but handed it to her advisor.

"Welcome, Lord Paulin," the Queen said, offering her palm. "May the Gods shine their light upon our time together."

"Indeed," he answered, taking her hand and boldly looking into her eyes. He held both her hand and gaze for just a moment longer than expected. Brindl looked past them to see Lord Yonda's lip curl slightly upward, as if he had just smelled something particularly rank.

From her position behind the princess, Brindl had an excellent view of the entire ceremony. She studied the faces of the players and tried to read their expressions, especially their eyes, despite the niceties that spilled from their lips. While these occasions were meant for false compliments and tedious, long-winded proclamations, Brindl determined she would take as much information back to Princess Xiomara as possible.

Twice she noted that the Castillian and Andorian regents' eyes locked and registered . . . what? Enmity? Scrutiny? If she'd not been on task, she'd have missed it entirely. The two men certainly knew each other, and if Brindl was correct, liked each other not at all. Surprised how exhausted she felt after standing and observing for hours, Brindl was relieved to finally scurry back to her tower when it was over. She longed to change into the clothes of an ordinary pigeonkeep and talk to Lili, who lit up her tower like a candle on the darkest night.

When entertaining guests of the palace, a lady's maid will limit her conversation to that of climate, food, and the arts.

—Ch. N. Tasca, *Palace Etiquette*

TEN

he following morning, after leaving
Lili in care of the birds, Brindl moved
through the halls as fast as she could
while still looking like a lady's maid,
rather than a servant. For Royals and
their attendants practically floated
between important destinations in their white clothes; the
benefit of jobs that used the mind rather than the hands,
Brindl decided.

It was time to tell Tonio as much of the truth as she could.
How will he react to my Moon Guild status and betrothal?
At yesterday's festivities, many servants had looked at her
with raised eyebrows. Even now, as she raced through the
palace, servants she'd crossed paths with dozens of times had
hesitated after a delayed recognition.

Oh, that I'm not too late!

Brindl reached the bakery and pushed open the heavy wooden doors. Many heads turned to watch, as if she were an apparition. Looking for Tonio, she finally spotted him at the end of the long work table. When he glanced up from rolling out dough, she could see in his eyes that she was too late. The bakery itself seemed longer than it had before, and Brindl's feet felt heavy as pearlstone as she approached him.

"Tonio, let me explain," she said, placing her hand on his arm. He stared at her hand, frozen in his task; she dropped it to her side.

"Explain what? I'm nothing but a common servant, I need no explanations."

Mama Rossi passed by and she could see the disappointment etched in her brow. The woman nodded but did not smile nor stop to embrace Brindl.

"Please, can we go someplace more private? I need . . . No, I *must* talk with you."

"Is that a command? I suppose I cannot refuse a direct order from a member of the court, a Moon Guilder no less."

"It's not like that. *Please*, Tonio. Let me explain."

"Fine. Follow me." Tonio walked to the back of the bakery and into the family's private room. How warm and inviting it had seemed that morning of her first visit. Now Brindl wondered if she'd ever be asked back. Tonio stood near the table but did not pull out a chair for either of them.

"Well?"

"I wanted you to hear it from me first," Brindl said, her voice quiet but steady. "I'm sorry, I didn't know how to tell you."

"Yes, I could see how it could be complicated for you," Tonio answered, turning away toward the window.

"It's not as simple as it appears," Brindl said, trying to start her explanation over. "Things seldom are."

"It looks simple to me. You left your guild behind to further your position in the palace."

"I did not do this for myself," Brindl answered, wrapping her arms around her gown, as if to protect herself from this charge.

"What servant wouldn't want to be lady's maid to a princess? Aren't you lucky to have such influential friends," he said, his eyes washing over her Moon Guild attire.

Brindl found herself annoyed then, anger crawling up her neck.

"And who are you to question my choices?"

"Your friend, I thought," Tonio said, "but you hardly even mentioned this Zarif to me."

"I didn't know how or what exactly to tell you." Brindl paused, searching for the right words "It wasn't really . . . a choice."

"How could your betrothal not be your choice?"

"I'm sorry," Brindl said quietly, "but I can't say."

"What do you mean?" Tonio's voice softened. "You should tell me."

Could she trust him? He seemed more upset than she'd expected. Perhaps she should leave all this behind. Dedicate herself to the princess and her new role. Certainly she could not reveal that it was the Diosa who moved her decision. But Brindl couldn't bring herself to walk away. Tonio was her friend. And she was a miner from Zipa, not some fluffy piece of cake in a bakery. She could make her own choices, and live with them.

"Princess Xiomara asked me to be her lady's maid. I could not refuse her."

"And the betrothal?" Tonio asked. Brindl dared not reveal more than she had. Already she was getting dangerously close to the precipice.

"Only Moon Guilders are accepted in the royal court." She looked past his shoulder and out the window into the hazy light of early morning on the mountain. "It was a necessity."

"I want to show you something," Tonio said, turning and opening a door. "Will you follow me?"

Brindl nodded.

Tonio led them through the door and down a passageway.

"This is how we transfer large cakes to the palace in case

of poor weather," he said, as if that explained where they were going.

Brindl followed silently as they wended their way through a series of smaller and darker passageways that connected the bakery to the palace kitchens. It reminded her of the salt mines, only less inviting, perhaps due to Tonio's mood. Finally, he stopped and opened a small unobtrusive door. Once inside, he lit a few lanterns and Brindl stood in awe.

Inside the small room were a dozen pearlstone sculptures of every size, from the smallest of birds to an enormous packhound. Brindl leaned forward to observe the details on the delicate bird sculpture, a fledgling taking its first leap into the air off an elegant twig. Elsewhere in the room were busts of various people and two sculptures of the palace itself, one small and the other quite large.

"This is my secret, Brindl," Tonio finally said, standing behind her as she studied the larger palace sculpture.

"*You* made these?"

"I did."

"You're quite talented," Brindl said, turning around to face him. "You must know that."

Tonio shrugged. "Does it matter? Most of my work gets eaten."

"But these are not cakes! They are amazing works of art."

"And yet, I bake cakes."

"I'm sorry, Tonio," Brindl replied, not knowing what else to say.

"My own father was as fine an artist, better even than anyone in Tequende, and yet he was forced to be a baker to marry my mother."

"I thought it romantic when your mother told the story."

"That's not how I see it."

Obviously. But hadn't Angelo Rossi made his own choice? Hadn't he made a life for himself and young family? Brindl didn't say it aloud lest she shatter this new peace.

"Don't you see?" he said. "I want to make art even though I was born an Earth Guilder. I want choices. As it was meant to be."

"You should have that choice," Brindl said, though she knew it was not so.

Tonio nodded, brushed off some dust from the palace sculpture. "Can you meet me tomorrow night at twelve bells in the garden?"

Brindl tilted her head. "I suppose, but why so late?"

"I have some friends I want you to meet. Don't be seen leaving the palace."

"Why the secrecy?"

Tonio gave her a sad smile. "Don't you remember? I have to keep some secrets so you'll come back again."

Brindl nodded. "Then so I shall."

———

That afternoon, Brindl sat in yet another courtyard that she hadn't known existed. *How many people serve their whole lives in this palace and never see the entire structure?* It was a beautiful day for the Queen's planned festivities for the regents. Parlor furniture had been brought outside and the royal court mingled in small groups with the regents and other honored guests of the Queen.

A quintet in the corner played just above a whisper on wooden flutes and stringed instruments. A banquet of treats stretched down one whole wall where one of the Rossis' sculptured palace cakes towered over the table as the center-piece, surrounded by other delicate pastries, sweetmeat pies, and breads. Dozens upon dozens of dishes lined the tables, the best the realm had to offer, and more than they could ever eat. Brindl remembered the piles of donated food at the Fray and wondered how many Quarry families could be fed by this lavish feast. *Such a waste!*

Brindl sat primly on the edge of her chair, trying to pick up on each nuance that passed between the guests without seeming to do so. Lord Yonda appeared before her, his plate laden with dozens of samples from the buffet. He bowed slightly. "May I join you, Lady . . . ?"

"Brindl," she answered, and bowed her head. "Of course, Lord Yonda," she continued, suddenly nervous. She had not yet had occasion to speak directly with either regent until now.

At first the regent was quiet, sipping his ale and munching not as politely as Brindl would expect from a man of his refinement.

"It is my custom to try everything before I make a final selection," he said, wiping his mouth on a kerchief, pulled from a velvety purple overcoat.

"How wise of you," Brindl said, with a smile and a nod. *Enough for two meals on his plate already.*

She had to admit, the man did know how to take great pleasure in his food. Mama Rossi would approve, Brindl thought, watching him. His eyes lit up his large pasty face with each new bite. Around half a century or so in age, dark spots dotted his face and the pate of his bald head, though only a few wrinkles marked his eyes. *Perhaps his skin has been filled in by sweets and creams.*

When he finished off the last morsel, he licked his thumb appreciatively and said, "Such extraordinary options. The best I've ever sampled, easily."

"I'm so pleased you like our fare," Brindl said. "The sweets are a specialty."

The regent leaned toward Brindl. "I'm not the only regent who enjoys the charms offered in the courtyard."

Brindl followed his gaze, which settled on Lord Paulin tucked beside Queen Twenty-two on a small couch, his sharp good looks striking even from a distance. Just then, the Queen's face flashed pleasure at whatever he'd said, their heads bent together companionably. Lord Yonda raised his eyebrows at Brindl, as if to confirm his observations. Obviously, lady's maids were not the only ones sent to observe.

"Brindl, tell me, what do you love most about Tequende?" he asked then, changing the subject.

It was an interesting question. Brindl thought carefully over her answer.

"I've never been elsewhere for comparison, but I love her people most of all," she replied. It wasn't quite true. She loved the people of her own guild the most, but she couldn't say something so divisive.

"All of the people or only some of them?" the regent asked, looking at Brindl with a bit of a challenge. He seemed to have read her mind.

"Whatever could make you pose such a question?"

"I do not like most people," he said, laughing. "I find them tedious at best."

Brindl joined him in his laughter, amused by his revelation. "An odd position for you as regent, I should think."

"Too true, too true," he said, then slapped his own knee, still chuckling. "But my father and his before him served as Castillian emissaries, so . . ."

"It was expected," she finished.

"But we were discussing Tequende." He smiled. "How cleverly you got me to reveal something of myself."

"And what do you love most about New Castille?" Brindl asked, truly interested in his answer.

"The food," he said, patting his large stomach.

Brindl grinned. He really was quite charming, and she liked his self-deprecation.

"Is this music to your tastes?" he asked, nodding toward the quintet, still plucking away on their instruments.

"It is a traditional sound, favored by the Royals."

"Obviously so, but that, my dear, is not what I asked. Do *you* prefer it?" He squinted his eyes at her once more, daring her to answer honestly.

"I . . ." Brindl started, then coughed behind her hand to buy time. She decided to be honest. "I prefer something more lively."

"Yes! Finally, an answer that is truthful rather than polite. How I hate polite banter, worse than a bedbug in your drawers." He chuckled heartily and took a giant swig of ale.

Despite her reservations, Brindl found herself enjoying the picnic and Lord Yonda's company.

A storyteller stepped onto a small stage then, and Brindl leaned forward. From her experience so far, storytelling seemed like an infrequent pastime in the royal city compared to Zipa, where most nights were spent around a fire retelling the godtales or spinning stories, each one more fantastic than the last.

The Moon Guild storyteller was older but not old, not beautiful nor ugly, plain of face and hair. But when she lifted her hands, the audience hushed. As she began recounting the birth of Tequende, her face transformed and her eyes became lit from within. Of all the godtales, the creation story was Brindl's favorite.

"In the beginning, Machué, our Mother Earth, found herself lonely, spinning through the dark night of eternity. So, she created the animals to live upon her wide apron, and for a long time, they offered solace and entertainment. Fox dug holes and tickled her. Raven braided her hair into fancy designs. Bear, when he wasn't sleeping in comfortable poses, played hide-and-seek.

"Still, Mother Earth wanted someone to share these lovely things with her. And so she decided, as many women do, to create children of her own. How content was Mother Earth preparing to be a mother of twins! To pass the time, she set about inventing things to amuse them: more animals, of course. Babbling creeks and rivers that led one to another for days and days for her children to explore. Vast caves and deep crevices with treasures tucked inside for their little fingers to discover. Mountains to climb so they would grow strong bodies. Art, music, weaving, and storytelling so they might find their own voices. Why, she almost forgot to give birth she was so busy!

"But one day, pain struck her down and she cried out. Tears sprung from her eyes. She cupped her hands to collect the tears and began mixing leaves, berries, and mud. With this she painted every living thing a new color to distract her from her labors. Finally, the twins were born: a son, Intiq, and a daughter, Elia. For many years the three lived happily together. But in the twins' fifteenth year, they became restless and kicked the shins of their mother for freedom and power of their own.

"And so, Mother Earth let them seek their destinies, those cherished children, as long as they promised her grandchildren. Although it would leave her own powers much diminished, she gave her son, Intiq, three amazing gifts: creativity, resourcefulness, and craftsmanship, and tacked him to the sky. She then pinned her daughter, Elia, to the night sky and blessed her with three more powerful gifts: wisdom, beauty, and art. Afterward, Mother Earth was left only with strength, humility, and steadfastness.

"All three created humans in their own image, and they became the People of Machué. Mother Earth made the most children to fill every pocket of her apron. With only their humble gifts to guide them, the Earth Guilders became the farmers and salt miners of the great land. They produced crops and tended their Mother's many animals, including packhounds, who became their guardians and companions.

"Next, Intiq created his own children, the Sun Guilders. Clever and enterprising, they became the traders and shop-keepers scattered across the realm entire. They prospered with lighter labors and enjoyed many hours of freedom under their father's warm face.

"Lastly, Elia created the children of the Moon Guild, and they were luckiest of all. For hers were the artists and poets, musicians and scholars, the rarest gems in the land. And from a handful of moonlit earth, Elia molded the Queen, human sister to the Moon Goddess herself, whom she set to rule over all the guilds.

"To preserve the realm and protect her from foreign enemies, every family of Tequende, every child of Machué, Intiq, and Elia, follows the Oath of Guilds, binding their second children in service to the Queen. So it was and shall always be."

The audience clapped politely but appreciatively, includ-ing Lord Yonda. Brindl thought it a lovely rendition of the story, told with more elegance than she was used to, though she hated to admit it.

"It's quite a clever fable," Lord Yonda remarked.

"Fable?" Brindl said, disturbed by his choice of words. "It's our most cherished godtale, the creation story of Tequende."

"Ah yes, a godtale that just happens to grant the Queen

an army of people duty-bound to serve her," Lord Yonda said, then patted Brindl's knee in a grandfatherly way. "Very clever. Very clever indeed."

Brindl blinked and sat back in her chair. Could a god-tale be sculpted for power and control? Unimaginable. And, yet . . . Yonda's words scratched like bedstraw inside her thoughts for the rest of the evening.

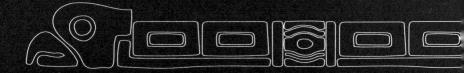

The vast majority of palace servants come from the Moon Guild, and are therefore trained in diplomacy and refinement. If you were born into the Earth or Sun Guilds, ensure that your bad habits do not follow you into the palace. Take your cues from the Moon Guilders around you, and leave your prior guild loyalties behind.

—Ch. N. Tasca, *Palace Etiquette*

ELEVEN

arkness didn't frighten Brindl; she had grown up amidst the dark and shadow of the mines. After all, a miner who was afraid of the dark was no miner at all. In the labyrinth underneath Machué's apron it often felt like the Sun God himself had been swallowed whole, so the dappled darkness of the forest was a comfort to Brindl, one she hadn't realized she'd missed.

Tonio attempted to move quietly along the narrow path, but made more noise than a wild boar, he was so unused to the dark. The moon was bright but the foliage dense, keeping them nearly hidden under the canopy of trees. A slim branch whipped back and Brindl caught it with her hand, though it stung her palm like a switch.

Meanwhile, Tonio had not spoken since they'd left the palace grounds. He'd kept secrets and surprises before but this felt different. Ominous almost.

Finally, they came to a clearing in the woods. Here, with the face of Elia looking down on them, Tonio paused. The stillness was full of anticipation—even the night birds and insects were quiet. Brindl sensed they were not alone, though she could see no one.

"I need to ask you for an oath of silence to Machué," Tonio said, turning toward Brindl.

"Why?" She did not like oaths.

"Please trust me, Brindl."

"Fine. It is yours." She clasped her hands and placed them over her heart. "I swear by our mother Machué to stay silent of all I see and hear."

Out of the shadows stepped a giant man, his bald pate gleaming in the moonlight. His arms were unnaturally large and twisted with muscles, like the stumps of two great trees. As he cleared the distance between them in a few long strides his face looked intent on Brindl, as if he was already trying to judge her contribution.

Tonio nodded toward the man. "This is Moth. He leads us."

Brindl recognized his nickname as Lili's uncle, the famous undefeated quarry fighter. He certainly looked big enough to squash anything or anyone in his path. He offered a massive, calloused palm to Brindl, and she felt like a child placing her small hand on his. After they broke apart, dozens of others suddenly emerged from the cloak of trees, like ants swarming from the ground.

"Brindl Tacora of the Zipa Salt Miners, these people, your people, have come together to right a wrong in Tequende," said Moth, his voice as deep and dark as the forest.

Brindl looked around her and nodded at everyone there. Though she could barely make them out among the shadows, she saw both men and women in the group, mostly Earth Guilders judging by their hair and dress, but even, she thought, a few Sun and Moon Guilders.

"We are not only quarry workers, but servants and farmers, maids and miners, and those who would ally themselves with our cause. All over Tequende, people are beginning to demand justice."

"What type of justice?" Brindl asked, still trying to make sense of these people, and why Tonio had brought her here.

A woman stepped forward. She was not much older than Brindl.

"The type of justice that does not disgrace a woman when she's been taken advantage of by someone with power."

Tonio leaned into Brindl and whispered, "She was sent home from the Alcazar pregnant and disgraced by Telendor."

"Telendor is gone," Brindl said, louder than she meant.

"But the power he used against her is not," Moth answered, folding his arms across his chest. "Until there is equality and respect among the guilds, among the members of those guilds, the children of Machué will continue to suffer injustices like hers, and worse."

An older man spoke next. "It is a disease eating at the flesh of this realm. It must be cut out."

Moth added to the old man's words. "All across Tequende, our people are coming together, rising up to fight this injustice, to take back the Oath of Guilds and make it whole again."

Tonio turned back to face Brindl. "All people should be on equal footing, everyone appreciated and honored for their contributions. We Earth Guilders are no more than the slaves of Tequende."

Brindl shook her head. "We are not slaves. There are no whips, no chains that bind us."

"Spoken like a Moon Guilder." Tonio's voice took on an edge. "You'll be the one served now in your white gown."

Brindl took a step back, as if she'd been slapped. "I told you, Princess Xiomara herself asked me to serve the realm. It's not as if I could say no."

"Exactly. If you could not refuse, are you much better than a slave?"

It was a valid point, though Brindl still felt hurt by

Tonio's words and angry that he would say them in front of these people. It occurred to her now how interested he had always seemed in her palace friends, in her proximity to Princess Xiomara. Had he courted her friendship for this purpose?

"I am no Moon Guilder, but I was asked to serve the realm and I will," Brindl replied loudly, though her gaze remained on Tonio.

"But where lie your loyalties, Brindl? With those in white or those of your people?" Moth said, his voice quiet but intense.

Brindl turned to the huge quarryman and looked him in the eye, refusing to be intimidated by his stature. "My loyalties lie with Tequende. As should yours."

"We are no traitors to Tequende. But we are tired of being the *dirt* under the boot of others," Moth answered.

Brindl flinched at his words. Earth Guilders were often referred to as "dirts" by members of the Sun and Moon Guilds. It was not a kind term.

"Our Earth Guild ancestors have toiled for this realm under twenty-two Queens," continued Moth. "We have broken our backs, bloodied our hands, taken on the most difficult, filthy work of this land for centuries, yet profited the least from it. You know this, Brindl Tacora of the Zipa Salt Miners."

Brindl looked away. She could not argue with him. She *did* know it. Only too well.

"We need your help," Tonio said, putting his hand on Brindl's arm. She flinched, still unsure how she felt about this boy who'd put her in the middle of a firestorm.

"We're asking you to join our cause," Moth said. "We call ourselves the Shadow Guard."

"Even if I wanted to join your cause, I still have five more years of service as a second-born. What would you have me do?"

Tonio paused. "The Far World regents are in Treaty Talks with the Queen. . . ."

"I'm well aware of that. And?"

Moth continued. "We wish to know what goes on at these talks, which issues are being discussed. Anything the Queen says or does that might reveal her motives behind the regents' visit."

Brindl looked from one man to the other. "You want me to *spy* for you? On the *Queen*? This is madness!"

Brindl didn't know what else to say. They were asking her to do much the same as Xiomara and Jaden had. Yet it felt different somehow. Traitorous. She shivered in the thin white Moon Guild gown, a sudden chill jangling her nerves.

"The realm is at a crossroads," Moth said, "and Queen Twenty-two plays a game of chess with the Far World. We of the Shadow Guard do not wish to be pawns. Help us, Brindl. Help your people."

Brindl took a long breath. "I cannot. What you ask of me is treason," she said, turning away. Would Tonio lead her back to the palace now or would she need to find her own way? She took a few steps toward the path, ready to leave this behind her.

"Wait!" Tonio said.

"There is something else you should know," Moth said.

"Yes?"

"Your friend Ory was here."

Brindl's eyes narrowed. "Ory? From the salt mines?"

"He came with a very interesting message from the Diosa: *When danger nears, let Brindl be your eyes and ears.*"

Brindl stood like one of the great trees around her. Whatever could that mean? It was the exact same message that Jaden and Xiomara had received.

"I don't know what to say," Brindl answered, the truth holding her steady. She truly *didn't* know what to say. Was Moth lying to her? Had someone spied on her conversation in the palace with Jaden and the princess? What could the Diosa mean by having her enmeshed with two opposing sides completely?

"Ory also brought this." Moth reached into his shirt and pulled out a white pendant, which hung from a leather string. A pendant made of salt. The sign of the Diosa. Brindl recognized it well.

"And this." Tonio took a piece of parchment from his pocket and handed it to Brindl. It was a drawing of Boulder. "He wanted you to have it."

So they are telling the truth.

Brindl waited a moment longer. She was a fly caught in a web much larger than her own understanding. She looked down at the drawing in her hand.

"Tell me what I need do," she said.

Moth nodded his approval, and though he didn't smile, his eyes held a warmth that surprised her.

"First you must take our oath."

"As the Diosa says, I will do."

"Kneel then, and repeat the words of the Covenant of Shadows."

All in the company surrounded Brindl and Moth, crossing their arms and holding the hands of those next to them. As Moth intoned the oath, Brindl's voice added to the chorus, repeating his words. She did not know what she was getting into precisely, but she would stand by her people.

I will speak truth.
I will seek justice.
I will protect the weak.

I will champion the righteous.
I will tend Mother Earth.
I will labor under Intiq.
I will dream under Elia.
I will serve my realm
According to my gifts
. . . In all things not contrary to the Gods.
For Tequende!

The next afternoon, Brindl tried to stifle her feelings of disloyalty. Gathering information for the Shadow Guard felt like a betrayal, but working for the Diosa, necessary. *I'm here to serve the spiritual leader of the Earth Guild, not the boy who bakes cakes.* As she listened to the Queen speak, she brushed the thoughts out of her head to take notes, but this time for an entirely different purpose.

"The journey to Lake Soga is not up for debate," said the Queen.

"But you'll be providing our enemies with a map of the realm. They'll be able to evaluate our defenses, recognize our weaknesses," Xiomara argued. "You'll compromise our security."

"We defeated Telendor's mercenaries with little more than youngsters guarding the gate. The Far World monarchs have not once dared trifle with my Second Guard army under all the Queens before me, nor will they do so now. They wish our trade, not our realm."

"I respectfully disagree, Your Majesty," Xiomara said, her voice tight. "We are directly in the middle of two sworn enemies, and we are no small prize with our salt and gold."

"Indeed, we are the gem of the Nigh World, the last empire run by its native royalty. The regents will see our land and people at their finest. Everything they see will impress them. They will know us, respect us, and trade fairly with us."

"But—" Xiomara started.

"We leave in three days' time." The Queen stood then and glanced at Brindl. "Bring your new lady's maid. Lord Yonda has taken a liking to her."

Brindl bit the inside of her cheeks and tried to keep her face neutral as Queen Twenty-two swept out of the room, her attendants following meekly behind.

Xiomara looked apologetically at Brindl, then addressed the much smaller assembly once the doors had closed. "It seems we will be going on a journey soon, whether we like it or not. I will greatly depend on each of you."

"We will not disappoint," Zarif said, while Tali, Chey, and Brindl nodded their agreement.

The discussion then turned to logistics of the trip and how they should prepare for it. They would be traveling by boat caravan along the Soga Tributary all the way to Lake Soga on the eastern range of Tequende.

"Tali and Chey, you'll need to determine how best to protect Xiomara on board, as well as how to stay alert for possible trouble along the banks of the river," Zarif remarked.

As the party continued to discuss safety issues, Brindl turned over her own preparations. I suppose I should alert the Shadow Guard, let them know the Royals and regents will be traveling soon, she thought, wondering when she might slip out to see Tonio next.

"Brindl?"

Brindl looked up and quickly composed herself. "I'm sorry, I was just thinking of how I might request some extra help at the aviary during my absence."

"Of course," said Xiomara. "We all have much to do and quickly. Brindl, you've made good progress with the Castillian regent, Lord Yonda, but I need you to continue. Charm him as best you can. We need to determine his intentions, if possible."

"I'll do my best," Brindl said, relieved when Xiomara's attention turned to Zarif.

"Zarif, I must remind you, apparently," the princess said, lifting her hands in a gesture that looked exasperated, "that Brindl is your betrothed."

Zarif's face showed shock, and he coughed into his hand. "Of course, I . . ."

"Is there not a book in your great library you could consult on these matters?" Xiomara continued. It was obvious the princess was now openly teasing Zarif, and Tali and Chey stifled laughs behind their hands. Zarif's face neared the shade of a nightflower, almost purple.

"Forgive me, friend," Xiomara added, placing her hand on his arm and patting it, "but your betrothal would appear more believable if you spent more time with Brindl rather than your books."

Zarif nodded his understanding and flashed a sheepish smile at Brindl, who shrugged sympathetically and smiled back. The princess had a point, and Brindl had grown tired of his avoidance.

Matters then turned to less humiliating subjects and Xiomara's voice resumed a more royal authority as they discussed the inordinate expense the upcoming river journey would require. How difficult it would be to prepare meals and entertainment that would satisfy the Queen and regents under the limitations of the river caravan. Unbeknownst to Xiomara and company until that very day, the Queen had commissioned a luxurious ship for the occasion of the regents' visit, as well as two smaller boats to accommodate Xiomara's retinue and the plentiful stores and servants needed for such a journey.

Brindl wondered how the people of Tequende would feel about seeing these luxury ships sail through their lives. Would it be a reminder of all they lived without? Or would they be proud of their Queen? Brindl did not know, nor whether she would be able to determine the truth in her people's eyes, if not their actions. Certainly the realm's merchants would be grateful for the extra business the voyage would provide. But would any of the money being tossed about end up in the hands of the people who worked hardest for the Queen's leisure and entertainment?

Brindl remembered Moth's words. *Not likely.*

Royals and palace attendants will frequently offer nonverbal commands to servants to conserve their energy and thoughts for more pressing matters. For example, a glance at the tea cart should be all that is required for a servant to pour refreshment.

—CH. N. TASCA, *Palace Etiquette*

TWELVE

hree days passed by in a flash of preparation. Lili's older sister, Farra, had joined her in the aviary to help with the birds and to stay while Brindl was away. Though Brindl was glad Lili would not be alone in the tower as she had been, it still felt strange to hand over her little sanctuary to them. She realized how attached she'd become to the place already: her shelf of books, her tidy kitchen, her own bed.

"I hear you are betrothed to Princess Xiomara's counselor," Farra said, as Brindl packed the last of her things. "My congratulations."

"Betrothed? You are betrothed?" Lili had said, jumping up and down, spilling birdseed from her apron in a fan around her feet. "You haven't told me about a counselor! What about your sweetboy from the bakery?"

"I told you, Lili, the boy from the bakery is only my friend."

"But who is this boy you will marry?" Lili's eyes lit up and a smile spread across her open face. "And when will you marry him? What is his name?"

Brindl wondered about this girl who thought so much of boys. She really must teach Lili to read so they could talk about *ideas* from time to time.

"Brindl? Where are you? Thinking of kissing him?" Lili giggled, then bent down with a brush to sweep the seeds from the floor.

Brindl reached for the dustpan to help her. "His name is Zarif, and he's my friend from the Alcazar."

"Was he a pigeonkeep like you?"

"Not at all, he was training for the Guard, and one of the best pledges there. He and I shared a friend, a great man, in fact." Brindl's voice caught with the memory. "His name was Saavedra. He taught me how to read, how to think. He was the best person I ever knew."

"But what of your betrothed? What do you like most about him?"

Brindl considered the question. "Zarif is very smart and very curious. And he's kind. Mostly."

"Does he have a handsome face? And big arms? I like big arms, they give better squeezes."

"Oh, Lili. How about I finish packing now and you sweep?"

A few minutes later, Brindl grabbed her bag and prepared to leave.

"I'll help you carry your things to the boat," Lili said.

"I think it best you stay with your sister and the birds."

"But then I won't see the caravan! Or your betrothed!"

"You are relentless, Lili," Brindl said, shaking her head. But in the end, she'd allowed the girl to accompany her. Lili scooped up Brindl's bag and skipped along beside her to the palace dock.

The three boats waited in a line: the Queen's first, then Xiomara's, and finally, the supply boat, though the Queen's vessel dwarfed the others at twice their height and length.

"Just look at them!" Lili exclaimed, bouncing up and down again. "Are you not so very excited? Tonight you'll be rocked to sleep by the river!"

"I can pretend I'm a tradeboat girl, like my friend Tali."

"What about me?" Tali asked, suddenly appearing behind them in her formal Guard uniform.

"I was just explaining to Lili here that you grew up on a tradeboat," Brindl said.

"Hello, Lili." Tali smiled at the girl and offered her palm. "I'm well pleased to meet you."

After the formal press of hands Lili said, "A tradeboat girl *and* a Second Guard warrior. You must be the most exciting person I've ever met!"

Tali laughed and mussed the girl's hair.

Brindl saw Zarif move toward them, careful to place his crutches just so along the slippery wooden dock.

"Tali and Brindl, we're near ready to depart," he said. "And who do we have here?" he added, nodding at Lili, who beamed at him.

"This is Lili, my new pigeonkeep apprentice," Brindl said, placing her arm around the girl's shoulders. "Lili, meet Zarif."

"Your betrothed!" Lili gasped. "Why, he's handsome as a godtale prince!"

Tali and Brindl laughed, while Zarif looked pleased and embarrassed at the same time.

"It is nice to meet you, Lili," he said finally, offering his palm to her. Lili slid her hand on Zarif's without taking her eyes off him, instantly smitten.

"Lili, it's time you're off to the birds," Brindl said.

"And you to the boat!" Lili answered. "I'll miss you much!" She squeezed Brindl hard and fast around the waist, then raced back to the palace.

The three friends stood there watching her zig and zag through the crowd toward the servant village.

"Isn't she a bundle of lightning," Zarif said.

"And words," Brindl added, their eyes meeting in a genuine smile for the first time since the betrothal had been announced.

Brindl tidied her braided hairstyle, hoping it looked decent enough to pass for a Moon Guilder, then climbed out of the tiny chamber and up a long ladder to the deck. Fog still skimmed the surface of the river and Intiq had not yet found his way over the mountains to warm the valley below. Brindl inhaled deeply, pleased to be among the fresh air again. How quickly she had grown accustomed to her rooftop tower and expansive views, and how claustrophobic in comparison the small cabin she now shared with the princess was.

A slight breeze tickled Brindl's neck and made her chill, but she was loath to go back down below to grab her shawl. Instead she tucked her hands into the pockets of her gown and wished for a cup of coffee. It was as if she'd summoned it.

"Coffee and a sweet?" asked a servant girl behind her, offering a tray of steaming mugs and breakfast cakes nestled inside scraps of lace. Brindl recoiled, remembering Tonio's hurtful words: *You'll be the one served now in your white gown.*

She tried to hide her discomfort and smiled at the girl. "With gratitude." She plucked a coffee and sweet from the tray and bowed slightly.

The servant girl, caught by surprise, ducked her head and scurried off across the deck.

Brindl stood at the railing and savored the warmth of the coffee as it spread through her limbs, then dipped the cake into it. Its crispy, delicate layers melted on her tongue, while its coating of pulverized sugar floated to the surface of her coffee and sweetened it.

The delicious treat made her think of Tonio and Mama Rossi. Surely their hands had created it? Were they on board the supply boat with the other servants and cooks, or had they prepared cakes ahead of time for the journey?

Her hand absentmindedly slid over the letter sewn into the pocket of her gown. After she'd seen Tonio to apprise him of the Queen's travel plans, he'd found her the next day and given her the letter. It was a message from Moth to the leader of the Soga loggers, a man called Manco.

Brindl had not wanted to take it, but Tonio had reminded her of the Diosa's charge. Now Brindl could feel the letter pressing, almost burning with the secret it held, though she did not know what it said.

She heard the approaching click of Zarif's crutches and turned to greet him.

"Did you settle into your quarters?" she asked, as he joined her at the railing.

"Indeed," he said. "Chey and I are sharing a room, just like old days at the Alcazar."

"How fun! And will you stay up all night talking like you used to?"

"If Chey's snoring counts as talking, then I suppose so," Zarif joked, as the servant girl returned and offered him coffee and cake. Though he thanked her politely, it was obvious that Zarif was used to being served: the subtle nod of dismissal, the unhesitating way he chose off the tray.

Brindl watched the girl slip away again, like a wisp of smoke. Like a shadow. "You don't really see them, do you?"

"Who?" asked Zarif.

"Never mind," said Brindl, turning her attention back to the river. "So is your appearance by my side an attempt to appease Xiomara's demand that we look betrothed in public?"

"Currently, there is no public unless you count the fish and the birds." Zarif smiled, and Brindl finally relaxed next to him. "But I thought we might practice."

"Good thinking. And since we were once friends, it shouldn't be that difficult." As soon as she said the words she regretted them. The hurt was plain on Zarif's face.

"Once friends? I thought we were still friends, Brindl."

"Yes, yes, of course. We *are* friends," Brindl said, putting her hand on Zarif's arm, her fingers warmed by his skin. "I meant only that what do betrothed look like, if not friends?"

He nodded, but did not respond.

Things have changed, Brindl realized. Or maybe I'm the one who's changed. She let her fingers slip from his arm.

"What do you think of the Queen's ship?" she asked, trying to leave the uncomfortable topic behind.

"It is certainly meant to impress others," Zarif said, clearly relieved to be talking about ideas rather than relationships. Perhaps they were not so different after all.

"It seems so big she should hardly be able to float."

"It's all a matter of which type of wood is used and how they seal it. Sap of the cordillo tree usually gives the best results."

"Is that so?"

"Though I do wonder if they build the boats directly upon the water once their hulls are complete or whether they finish them on dry land."

"I'm sure you'll find out, or figure out which book to consult."

Zarif chuckled, in the easy way she remembered back at the Alcazar.

Perhaps we'll muddle through this after all.

All day the caravan floated down the Soga Tributary and villagers lined the banks to wave and cheer as she slid by. The Queen's ship, painted a pearly white, fairly glowed on the surface of the dark water. Though Tequendian tradeboats were traditionally multicolored, like the bright clothes of their Sun Guild owners, the Queen's vessel was as elegant and refined as she was, floating across the water like a white swan. The vast main deck had been designed for entertainment purposes, like dancing and large meals, and could connect by portable bridge to Xiomara's boat or the supply boat that brought up the rear.

At times Brindl caught sight of the Queen waving at the crowds, which pleased them immensely, but more often she ignored them while speaking to Lady Ona and the regents on the deck of her ship. Meanwhile, Princess Xiomara did her best to make amends by smiling and waving at the onlookers from the railings of her smaller boat.

When evening fell, the caravan docked in the village of Tibaso. Brindl once more climbed the ladder to the deck, trying not to trip over her new gown, easily the most beautiful thing she had ever worn. Made of fine brushed cotton in three different shades of white, the sleeves just covered her elbows then ruffled out like flowers. The dress's neckline scooped in front into a tight bodice, then flared at the hips and dropped to a jagged hemline near her ankles, showing off dainty beaded shoes. Brindl had pinned her hair high, and a few curls cascaded down her shoulders.

Zarif awaited her on the dock, handsome as always.

"You look lovely, Brindl," Zarif said, his eyes scrolling across her. "Like a true daughter of Elia."

Though meant as a compliment, his words made Brindl's

stomach knot. *But I am Machué's daughter and proud of it.* She resisted the urge to pull the pins from her hair, and the ribbons from her gown.

The rest of the royal party disembarked from their boats then, greeted by the village leaders, who had planned an evening of local food, musicians, and storytellers.

"Fair Brindl, how lucky I am to see you once more," Lord Yonda said, joining her as they stepped off the dock toward the festivities. Brindl's feet felt suddenly unsteady and she reached for Zarif, then quickly stopped herself, lest she knock him over. Lord Yonda grabbed her elbow.

"It is sea feet, my dear," he said.

"Sea feet?" Brindl asked.

"When you travel by boat for many hours your feet get used to holding your body against the movement beneath it. When you step upon dry land your feet wait for the waves."

"I wonder if my friend Tali ever suffers from it," Brindl mused.

"Why would it be different for her?" the regent asked. "She is one of Xiomara's guards, correct?"

"Yes, but she grew up on a tradeboat."

"Are you talking about me again, Brindl?" Tali asked, coming up from behind. "I seem to be a popular topic today."

"I was just telling the regent how you grew up on a tradeboat. We wondered if you ever suffered from sea feet."

"Never." Tali shook her head. "It's one of the benefits for certain."

"It must have been marvelous to grow up on a tradeboat, yes?" Yonda asked.

"The very best, sir," Tali answered, "though my family's boat—*Cora's Heart*, we called her—was much more modest than these."

"Of course, of course, she would be, yet equally charming, I'm sure. But you speak of her in the past tense. Why is that?"

Brindl glanced at Yonda in admiration. The man was about to glean an important detail of Tali's life by noticing something as simple as one word in the past tense.

"Our tradeboat was destroyed in the Battle for the Alcazar."

"I'm so sorry," the regent said. "I hope your family has recovered its living."

"The Queen provided new tradeboats for those that were sacrificed during the battle," Tali answered.

"And this new tradeboat, is she much like your old one?"

Tali paused. "She suffices."

Yonda nodded, his face thoughtful. "Sacrifices are not easily replaced." He paused then and glanced down at Brindl's Moon Guild attire. "Nor are new things always better than the old. But come now, ladies, let us put away sad thoughts and see if they know how to cook in Tibaso."

The Queens of Tequende do not marry or have children, but may take consorts for entertainment and delight. A royal consort must be given the utmost deference and regard, as one of three chosen intimates of the Queen. As such, the consort shall not be subject to speculation or gossip within or outside the palace walls.

—CH. N. TASCA, *Palace Etiquette*

THIRTEEN

ive little girls stepped onto the makeshift stage dressed in clean and simple Earth Guild tunic and trousers, though inked designs scrolled up their hands and arms to mark the occasion, as if it were the Festival of Light. A small band began to play, the music reminding Brindl of the tunes played at home, and though she yearned to clap along like the villagers, she pressed her hands together like the other Moon Guilders in her company. The five girls began to dance and twirl, their feet playfully catching the rhythm of the band.

Brindl, sitting behind Queen Twenty-two and Lord Paulin, watched him lean in for the third time and whisper in her ear. The Queen fiddled with the lace on his cuff, then glanced up at him through her lashes, as if he were the fourth god of Tequende. Though the Queens of Tequende were not allowed husbands, there was no such prohibition on lovers. Brindl wondered if the Queen had already taken Paulin as her consort. An intimacy and easiness marked each interaction between them, their hands finding more subtle excuses to touch each other since the last time Brindl had seen them together.

Lord Yonda, on the other hand, seemed entranced by the performance, clapping his hands in time with the drummer and smiling encouragingly at the nervous girls. When the performance ended, the Queen's party clapped politely and shifted in their small chairs, but Yonda cheered the young girls, whose faces lit up like lanterns at the applause. Brindl found herself liking Yonda even more for his generosity of spirit.

After the dancers came a storyteller, a trickster of the hand, and a panpipe ensemble to end the evening. The panpipers played a song of such longing and home that Brindl found herself swept back once more to Zipa, where she pictured her brother, mother, and father sitting around their plain table sharing the day's news and a small meal of grain and root vegetables from the garden. How long would it be before she could go home?

The Queen looked relieved when the humble performances

finally ended. The stage was reset with a large table covered in the traditional woven cloth and design of the region, interlocking diamonds in bright jewel tones. Small lanterns suspended from rope were strung above the table. Brindl hoped the hours they spent seated in conversation would prove useful to Xiomara's cause. Tali had taken a knife for the princess; perhaps Brindl's eyes and ears could prevent one.

At first, it was just another polite meal. Foods of the region were trotted out one at a time, prepared by local cooks to showcase their most spectacular dishes. How different the food tasted here than at home or in Fugaza. The meat course was presented on skewers with roasted vegetables between them, their savory flavor complemented by chunks of Lana fruit.

The conversation mainly focused on the earlier presentations, but after the third course, a cold green soup with swirled cream, words between the two regents became heated. Though Brindl had only caught snatches of their conversation prior, their voices now rose and came with a sharp edge.

"It was your monarch, not mine, that broke the Treaty of Cordova," Yonda said, as a slab of spiced meat was set before him. It was the way he cut into it, with decisive strokes, that revealed his true feelings while his face remained placid, overtly polite, Brindl decided.

"Never," Paulin answered, gesturing to a servant for more wine. "We all know my Queen did no such thing. It was a snake inside Tequende itself that orchestrated the attack on the Alcazar."

"In Andorian ships with Andorian warriors?" Yonda challenged, his knife poised above his meat to attack again.

Surprisingly, the Queen remained neutral as the two parleyed. She looked at both as they spoke, but her face revealed nothing. Brindl noticed that Tali and Chey took a step closer to the table. Princess Xiomara remained silent. Lady Ona and Lord Paulin held a glance for just a beat too long. *Or did they?*

"Captain Telendor bought them with gold," Paulin answered after swallowing another gulp of wine. "Loyalty often can be."

"Do you think so?" the Queen asked casually, as if it were not about her own realm they were discussing, but an interesting philosophical question.

Lord Yonda was the first to answer. "I'd venture to say that *men* can be bought, but loyalty nay. Perhaps you might explain, Your Majesty, why you named Telendor's own son, Jaden, as the new Queen's Sword? It seems an . . . interesting choice."

"He is the best," she answered, dabbing her mouth with a napkin. "I only tolerate the best."

Brindl saw that Tali was now intently following the conversation, her eyes unable to tear themselves away. Meanwhile, Chey stood with his arms across his broad chest, constantly scanning the hall for hints of a threat.

"Do you not worry that he will follow his father's path and he, too, will betray you?" Yonda asked. The entire party seemed to pause in their meal, utensils poised mid-bite, glasses frozen at their lips.

"No more than I worry about you," she answered, smiling with her lips but not her eyes. "Or Lord Paulin. And yet, you've both assured me of your peaceful intentions toward my realm. The Treaty of Cordova, signed by my predecessor, Queen Twenty-one, and your sovereign monarchs still stands, does it not?"

Lord Yonda looked amused. "Indeed, Your Majesty," he said, turning back to his food with gusto.

"Though peace treaties are notoriously broken," replied Paulin, stabbing a piece of meat. "Now a marriage, on the other hand, is often a much more reliable alliance."

"I have considered this possibility," the Queen replied, swirling the dregs of wine in her glass.

"I thought the Queens of Tequende did not marry, Your Majesty," Lord Yonda said, raising his brow, "though 'tis a pity for all mankind."

"I did not mean me," Twenty-two answered, looking

across the table, "but Princess Xiomara would make a generous offering of goodwill to either realm, I should think."

Princess Xiomara's posture stiffened, her face registering shock before she could mask it.

"I'm sure the prince heir to Castille would be more than interested in such a lovely offer," Lord Yonda said, bowing his head to Xiomara. "We would be honored to align ourselves with the great Tequende."

"As would Andoria," Lord Paulin said loudly, trying to hide the irritation in his voice. "My Queen's heir and nephew, Prince Ricardo, will soon come of age and be in want of a wife."

"Another possibility worth considering," said Twenty-two, raising her glass. "To alliances."

"Will you follow me, Brindl? Help me dress for bed?" Xiomara said much later that night.

"Of course," Brindl answered, stifling a yawn. She almost felt more exhausted than after a day in the mines. As elegant as her new dress was, she couldn't wait to shed it and slip into her narrow bunk to read.

Xiomara said nothing else until they were inside her room, the door closed tightly behind them. The princess reached up and pulled a pin from her hair and scratched at the spot underneath. It was an ordinary action, certainly, but

Brindl realized she'd never seen the princess do anything like it before.

"That's been pinching my scalp all evening," Xiomara said. "I thought I'd never get to take it out."

"Shall I brush your hair?" Brindl asked, knowing this is what a lady's maid was supposed to do, but still uncertain of her role. The princess had any number of lady servants to help with her hair and dress in the palace, but here on the boat, there was only one other maid.

"Would you?" Xiomara dropped into a small chair in front of her dressing mirror, as if she were melting.

"You have beautiful hair, Princess," Brindl said, her fingers loosening the pins and unraveling the complex braids.

Princess Xiomara nodded but did not respond to the compliment itself.

"My maid Kalla could do this, but I wanted to talk to you alone. I hope you don't mind."

"Of course not. I am your lady's maid, after all."

"Yes, well," Xiomara said, reaching for a moist towel left for her use, "that was not the original plan."

"The original plan?" Brindl asked, her fingers snagging on a knot in the princess's hair. She reached for the comb and gently pulled it loose.

"Yes, the original plan was for you to be counselor to me alongside Zarif," Xiomara said. "Saavedra thought you would offer me great insight into the Earth Guilders of the realm."

"He told you this?" Brindl asked, incredulous.

"We discussed it at length in our letters," Xiomara said, wiping her face with the damp rag, erasing the kohl around her eyes, "but your very Earth Guild status prevented it."

"I am honored he thought me worthy of such a role," Brindl said, smoothing the princess's long hair into a shiny black waterfall.

"He was a wonderful tutor, but he caught the ire of the Queen," Xiomara said, sighing. "She banished him to the Alcazar as a lowly pigeonkeep because he told her the truth rather than what she wanted to hear."

Brindl tried not to be a bit smarted by the words "lowly pigeonkeep." It was, after all, her own position.

"I was lucky to know him," Brindl said, "but his talent was wasted tutoring me and holding court for Second Guard pledges."

"He didn't think so," Princess Xiomara said. "Brindl, would you call me Xia? It was what Saavedra called me. I'd like to hear it spoken again."

"I will try . . ." Brindl hesitated, and smiled at the princess in the mirror. "Xia."

"The Guild system does have its limitations," Xiomara said, dabbing her finger in a small jar and smoothing the cream over her lips. "It seems unfair that you should be excluded from my counsel due to your birth."

"Each of us has a role to play," Brindl replied, considering her words. It seemed unthinkable that a Royal might actually consider what it might be like to be an Earth Guilder. Yet Xiomara just had. She wished she could speak freely to the princess, tell her about the concerns of the Shadow Guard. But she had sworn an oath of silence to Machué.

"Apparently *my* role is to be sold off to the highest bidder," Xiomara said, a flash of anger crossing her face.

"Would she do it?" Brindl asked.

Xiomara stood and gestured for Brindl to help her unhook the gown. It spilled off her shoulders into a heap on the floor. She looked so tiny without it on, so small in stature compared to the Queen.

"She would like nothing better than to be rid of me."

"But you are next in line for the crown," Brindl said, handing the princess her nightgown. She grabbed the fallen dress from the floor and carefully draped it over a nearby chair.

"Exactly why she'd sell me off, so she could replace me with a new Queen-in-Waiting who will do her bidding. It was definitely a threat for me to hold my tongue."

"Well, she can't exactly make you a pigeonkeep," Brindl said.

The princess laughed, then dropped onto her bed, folding her legs up beneath her. She looked so young, her face so open. She patted the blanket for Brindl to join her. Brindl tried to act like this was just an ordinary girl from Zipa, sharing a festival night together, and not the future Queen of Tequende.

"Now you must tell me everything you noted tonight," Xiomara said.

And Brindl did tell her everything.

Almost.

A lady's maid shall always keep her emotions in check. A demure, measured response is always preferred to unseemly expressions of irritation, enthusiasm, or ire.

—CH. N. TASCA, *Palace Etiquette*

FOURTEEN

wo days later, the gallant procession of boats reached Lake Soga. Brindl and Zarif met early in the morning before the others started their day to share coffee and a few words alone. They spoke easily of the previous day's events and discussed how to get more information from both regents, if possible. But their conversation changed as the boat slipped from the river into the lake itself. It was like they'd been transported to a new realm.

The lake was large, though not as vast as Lake Chibcha in the south where they'd spent a year at the Alcazar in training. The early morning mists rolling across the placid waters made the bank of the far side invisible. Houses appeared to float over the lake like apparitions. Constructed on tall stilts, they reminded Brindl of shore birds on their skinny legs hovering over the water. A few of the houses even had fences partitioning off a part of the lake, like a yard of water. Inside the fences vegetables and flowers bobbed in the wake on a garden bed of mosslike plants.

As they neared, Brindl saw that the houses looked like they'd been pieced together from scraps and castoffs, with odd angles and half-chewed planks. Longboats had been tied up alongside many of the houses, their hulls stacked with cone-shaped baskets, which Brindl supposed were used to trawl for fish.

Zarif pointed to a man who balanced on the back of his boat and paddled with a long pole, while a large bird stood in silhouette on the prow.

"He fishes with a bird to balance his boat?" Brindl asked, for she thought it looked like something from a fractured dream.

"In fact, the bird does some of the fishing for him," Zarif answered. "Oh, how I have wanted to see Lake Soga since I first . . ."

"Read about it in a book?"

"You know me well, Brin." Zarif grinned, raising his hot coffee to his lips and blowing across its surface before sipping.

"But do tell me how the bird fishes for him."

"He ties a ribbon around the base of its neck so the larger fish cannot be swallowed."

"Genius! But if the bird does not get fed, why does he do it?" Brindl rubbed her arms, for gooseflesh had appeared on them. It was cooler on the open water than the protected banks of the river. Zarif removed a wrap from his shoulders and placed it around her. It was a kind gesture and she smiled at him appreciatively, murmuring her thanks.

"First, because the bird is raised to do it, much like our bluejackets are trained to come home. But the fisherman must also reward the bird."

"He feeds it out of his own hand, I suspect," said Brindl, "so the bird learns to depend on him and not his own work alone."

"That is exactly so. How did you know this?" Zarif asked, his face obviously surprised by her insight.

"It is how we train packhound puppies loyalty to their Earth Guild families," Brindl said, "though Machué teaches us to be kind masters over her animals."

"This makes sense to me," Zarif said, accepting another cup of coffee from a servant girl without pause, "as they are valuable assets to a family."

"They are more than family *assets*," Brindl replied. "They are family *members*."

Zarif shrugged. "I'm not sure I see the difference."

Brindl bit her tongue.

An hour later the whole boat was wide-awake and bustling about to prepare for the day. They'd arrived just in time for the Soga Games, an annual event in which the local fishermen invited the loggers from the neighboring forest to join them for a day of sport. Over the centuries, it had turned into a great rivalry, followed by a communal fish fry and celebration.

The fishermen were naturally small people but possessed amazing balance and coordination. The loggers were gigantic, or so they seemed in comparison, and relied on brute strength and endurance to survive. Both peoples were said to descend from the same great matriarch, whose twin sons had divided their inheritance fairly between them: one who loved the lake and the other the forest. The story told that because each of the twins had followed his heart, everyone prospered.

Princess Xiomara's boat skirted along the shoreline northward to the log-rolling event. Lord Yonda had joined them, as the Queen had decided to skip the morning's festivities, preferring to anchor her ship away from the noise and crowds.

Brindl was relieved she did not have to be in company

of the Queen that day, and nor so it seemed did the rest of Xiomara's party. After the intensity of last night's meal, it almost felt like they'd received a day off.

While Xiomara gave Lord Yonda a tour of the boat, Brindl sat with Zarif, Chey, and Tali in cushioned deck chairs as they traveled to the other side of the lake.

"I thank you again, Chey," Tali said.

Chey waved a hand as if to dismiss her thanks. "It was no trouble at all."

Zarif looked from one to the other. "What needs to be thanked, if I may ask?"

Tali's face lit up. "Chey arranged for a longboat to take me to the Soga floating market, where my family will be docked for the festivities. I can't wait to see my father and Nel."

"How fun for you, Tali," exclaimed Brindl, though she felt a twinge of envy. *Who in second-born service to the Queen would not?* Brindl had not seen her own family in over a year.

"My warmest regards to your family, Tali. I wish I could share in some of your twin's delicious treats," Zarif said.

"The Queen's own food does not satisfy your appetite?" Brindl asked, trying to lighten her own mood by poking Zarif a tad.

"You've never tasted Nel's food," Chey answered, a big

grin spreading across his face. "It's more noble and heartier than any palace fare." He pointed a finger at Tali. "You'd best bring some of it back if you know what's good for you!"

Just then, Princess Xiomara and Lord Yonda emerged from the upper cabin, and the four of them rose from their seats at attention. The princess nodded, and they made their way to the side of the boat, where servants had arranged a comfortable viewing area along the railing.

A short time later, the boat sailed into view of the first competition. The crowd, who had obviously been waiting for their arrival, cheered from longboats, platforms, and piers that jutted out around the competition ring. Babies were lifted onto the shoulders of their fathers to catch a glimpse of the princess, while a group of rowdy boys called and whistled to catch her attention. Xiomara smiled widely and waved to one and all, though Brindl noticed Tali and Chey scanning the crowd, alert for any faces painted in anger or cruel intent. To them a crowd meant chaos and an increased likelihood of danger.

The ring itself was a section of the lake circled by a floating fence. Inside, two men sat on a giant log facing each other, their feet dangling in the water like young children. A longboat floated nearby with two more men inside it. Like the pair on the log, it was obvious that one man was a fisherman, the other a logger, judging by their difference in size.

All of the men were baked a dark brown from days in the sun, as were the onlookers gathered to watch.

The fisherman stood in the longboat and blew through a large shell to quiet the crowd. He cupped his hands around his mouth. "The log roll competition shall begin."

The crowd roared its approval.

"The best three out of five wins the match. Men, stand and bow."

The two men scrambled upright onto the giant log, making the marked difference between them even more pronounced. The fisherman, wiry and thin, looked half the logger's size in every dimension, though he appeared more comfortable on the log, his toes pointed outward for better balance. The logger, an enormous specimen of a man whose neck looked like the stump of a tree, kept his giant feet pointed directly at his opponent.

Both men bowed, then the longboatsman drew the large shell to his mouth and blew it again.

At first the two men faced the same direction, to the mountains of the north, and slowly began rolling the log under their feet. It looked as though they were cooperating and not trying to throw each other off. The crowd began clapping slowly, in time with the rhythm of their feet. Then the fisherman jumped to face the opposite direction, changing the motion of the log. The logger tipped but did not fall. Then, with the strength of his enormous feet, the logger stopped the motion of the log and began spinning it once again toward the north. This time, it was the fisherman's turn to teeter, and he threw his hands up behind him like a bird landing in a nest. When he regained his balance, he dipped his foot into the water and kicked it into the logger's face, momentarily forcing him to close his eyes.

The fisherman switched positions again, an elegant dancer's motion, and began running in place on top of the log in tiny little steps. Brindl found herself holding her breath and clasping the railing of the boat. As the log moved faster and faster under the fisherman's command, the giant logger struggled to keep pace. His large feet were a burden, and he slipped and fell face-first into the lake. The fishermen in the audience roared their approval and the logger families cried, "Ohhhhhh!" Brindl longed to shout with them, but took her cues from the princess and clapped politely instead.

Everyone cheered as the victor helped pull his opponent back onto the log for the next round. This second ended more quickly than the first, with the fisherman again using his incredible sense of balance to his advantage. On the third round, however, the logger kicked a giant waterfall into the smaller man's face, knocking his balance enough that he tumbled to the end of the log and fell off. The logger families began clapping in unison, chanting the logger's name: "Toma! Toma! Toma!"

The fourth match was longest of all. The log switched

direction no less than half a dozen times, equally controlled by the two determined competitors, though Brindl sensed the smaller man was merely biding his time. Having spent all of their lives navigating the lake in longboats, the Soga fishermen clearly had the advantage in this competition. They knew how to stay on top of the water rather than in it.

"I believe the fisher will soon win this competition," Zarif said, echoing Brindl's thoughts.

"Agreed," she answered. The princess added her consensus, while Lord Yonda stood beside her, his mouth curled in what looked like a smirk.

"The people out here—all Earth Guilders, yes?—appear more"—Lord Yonda paused, obviously searching for words—"*native* than in the royal city."

Brindl wondered if it was the villagers' dark skin that made him say it or if it was their behavior itself, their loud, raucous enjoyment. Either way, she bristled at the less-than-subtle condescension.

"They do spend their days out of doors working, Lord Yonda," Brindl said, unable to control the tightness in her voice. She tucked a hand inside her pocket, feeling the secret letter from Moth there under an extra layer of fabric.

Yonda raised an eyebrow in her direction, an amused look on his face.

Black tunnels. He baited me on purpose to see if I'd reveal my feelings.

Lord Yonda smiled, almost in apology. "It would certainly make them appear more rugged," he agreed.

Finally, the fisherman unseated the logger one last time to both the great joy and disappointment of the mixed audience. When the logger reached up from the water to shake his opponent's hand, he pulled him into the lake and the fisherman's feet flipped over his head. Brindl gripped the boat railing. *Would this be considered an insult?* The fisherman came up laughing and sputtered into the logger's face.

The onlookers roared, all of them, as the men swam toward opposite piers where their families stood waiting for them. The fisherman was hoisted out of the water and carried above the heads of the crowd among laughter and laud. Hearty pats on the back greeted the logger as everyone made their way to a floating pavilion where fish fritters and mountain ale awaited them.

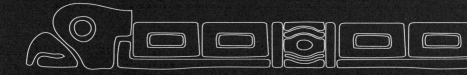

A lady's maid is often a Royal's most intimate confidante. As such, a lady's maid shall never discuss a Royal with anyone, lest she wish to immediately be relocated to the stables to serve the palace barn animals.

—CH. N. TASCA, *Palace Etiquette*

FIFTEEN

he Moon Guild gown dropped to the floor, looking like a puddle of cream. Brindl stepped over it carefully, then picked it up and hung it on a peg by her bunk. She pulled a humble Earth Guild tunic over her head and stepped into the skirt that matched it, both borrowed from a kind fishergirl she'd met earlier that afternoon. As her fingers tied the deep-pocketed apron around her waist, she smiled to herself. Not many girls would choose scratchy, rough-woven llama wool over fine, soft-brushed cotton, but Brindl was one of them. She felt more herself than she had in weeks. Spirits lifted, she looked forward to being an Earth Guilder again, at least for an evening.

Brindl hoped her Moon Guild slippers would survive the

trek up the mountain, but she had no further time to worry about it. She had to meet the fishergirl and her sister, who'd agreed to walk with her up to the festivities. Unleashing the fancy braids in her hair, she finger-combed it quickly. Just before she rushed up the ladder she remembered the purpose of her trip. *What kind of messenger can't even remember the message?* She took a letter opener to her gown on its peg, ripped open the pocket seam, retrieved the letter, and slipped it into her apron.

Just as she was about to leave the boat, Tali turned the corner and waved to Brindl.

"Have fun with your cousin!" Tali called.

"Thanks! Enjoy the night with your family," Brindl answered, turning away quickly to avoid any more lies. She felt terrible about deceiving her friends, but there had been no way around it. When Tali had invited them all to her family's tradeboat that evening, Brindl was surprised, almost mortified by how easily the lie came to her. The story of her cousin Amani's marriage to a logger slipped off her lips completely believable, without a hint of suspicion. It almost made it worse somehow. Where the falsehood or even the name Amani had come from, Brindl didn't know. But the best chance to deliver the message to Manco would be tonight, while everyone was distracted, and she looked forward to being rid of it.

The Moon Guild white slippers were a poor choice for

traveling up a steep, narrow mountain pass, and Brindl wished she'd thought to borrow some boots as well. She wondered how she would make them presentable in the morning, as every step put another layer of dirt upon their delicate surface. Oh well. One problem at a time. The fishergirls were kind, but Brindl tried to outmaneuver their curiosity.

"So are you a servant in the palace kitchens?" the older sister asked.

"No," Brindl answered, unsure of how much to reveal.

"Where then?" asked the younger sister, reaching for a branch as she climbed.

"The aviary," Brindl answered.

"It must be so exciting to work in the Queen's Palace," the younger one said, the mirror image of her older sister, just a size or two smaller.

"I suppose," Brindl said. "What's it like to live in a floating village?"

The younger sister, who obviously loved to talk as much as breathe, went on and on about being out on the water, helping their brother, training the magnificent fishing birds. It did not take much prodding to keep her talking all the way to the logger's village. Brindl was reminded of Lili, whom she suddenly missed. The older, quieter sister attempted to divert the discussion back to Brindl, but a few well-timed questions about training the fishing birds ended that. Brindl thought of Lord Yonda then, and his clever ability to steer conversations in the direction of his choosing. *I think he'd be quite proud of me right now.*

In less than an hour they reached the logger's village, which was just as amazing as Lake Soga's floating village. The trees themselves were beyond comprehension, so tall were they. Brindl craned her neck back but could still not see the tops of them. Ten logger men, with giant arms outstretched, would not be big enough to span their girth.

The cabins, built so that they became part of the trees themselves, looked like birdhouses tucked inside the natural hollows of the forest. Plank bridges crisscrossed between the cabins like spokes on a wheel, and connected in the middle, where an enormous covered platform hung suspended high above the ground.

"The trees . . ." Brindl said, in wonder.

"It is the Mother's Wood," the elder sister answered, "sacred to the loggers."

"I thought the Mother's Wood was a whimsytale," Brindl said, her voice just above a whisper. It seemed a holy place, where the Gods would walk.

"The first time you see it is the best!" the young one said, enjoying Brindl's delight.

"Why, just one of these trees could provide homes for an entire village," Brindl said, still craning her neck. "More perhaps."

"But the loggers only harvest those that die naturally,"

the older sister said, pointing at a fallen tree in the distance. "Machué provides for her own."

"Praise the Mother," Brindl answered, as the custom required, though more than ever the words resonated deep inside her. Humbled by the amazing forest, she forgot for a moment why she'd come.

"We need to find our friends," the older sister said, as they finally approached a great open-air pavilion among the trees. "Will you be fine from here?"

"Yes, thank you so much for your company," Brindl said. "I'm sure I can find my cousin now."

"Enjoy the dance!" the girls sang over their shoulders, then skipped off.

"I shall!" Brindl answered, and turned to scan the pavilion. The light was fading through the leaves and the patterns danced among the forest floor, as if practicing for the night's festivities. A six-piece band set up on a raised platform, while banquet tables slowly filled with piles of goodies and drinks as more people arrived. Brindl loved this, perhaps best of all, the way Earth Guild families would each cobble together ingredients for signature dishes and bring them to festivals for sharing. Food prepared by someone who loved those she made it for always tasted best, Brindl decided.

She looked around to see whom she might ask about Manco, but the crowd had already begun to circle around the pavilion floor, vying for the best spots to watch the dancers. Apparently, not only did the fishermen and loggers test their skills on the water, but on the dance floor as well. Brindl found herself swept up in the anticipation and decided that Manco would have to wait until later, as everyone's attention was now firmly occupied.

First up was a young logger couple who took to the dance floor like they'd been raised on it. The band played a tune that Brindl didn't recognize but was an obvious favorite of the crowd. The girl twirled and jumped in and out of her partner's arms without missing a single beat. Her plain Earth Guild clothes had been dressed up for the occasion, with fresh flowers pinned along the hem. The couple danced barefoot and sometimes their brown feet moved so fast it was hard to distinguish them from the wooden floor. When the music stopped, they bowed to each other, then the audience, and waved as they left the stage.

The next couple, obviously fisherpeople, danced to a slower piece, their moves fluid and graceful. Brindl was reminded of fisher birds, of wings opening and effortlessly taking flight. The way the two dancers looked at each other, their gaze never wavering, made Brindl feel wistful, almost lonely in the crowd of hundreds. The applause was more subdued, but equally respectful when they finished their lovely duet.

One more couple took the floor and Brindl was surprised when the male dancer was introduced as Manco. He and his partner were the last contestants. Though much taller than his companion, they shared the same wild, curly hair, and Brindl wondered if they were siblings. Again the band played a bright tune, one that Brindl recognized, a folksong played at weddings and sometimes the funerals of jolly people as well. The crowd came to life, clapping in time with the dancers' fast feet. Manco threw his partner around his body and over it, tossing her like a rag doll, as she called out to the audience, encouraging them to stomp their feet and sing along.

Brindl loved the whimsical moves and the obvious joy written on their faces, and she wasn't the only one. The judges had no difficulty awarding the prize to Manco and his partner. The crowd erupted in cheers. Then, the dancing began for everyone. Brindl saw her chance to get to Manco, hoping she could get him alone briefly to deliver the message. She wove through the tangle of people, careful to keep him in view as she made her way across the floor. Finally, she found herself face-to-face with the man.

"Manco?" Brindl asked, with a slight curtsy.

"That's me," he answered, smiling. He wiped a drop of sweat off his brow with his sleeve, then offered his palm to her.

Brindl slid a hand on top of his and introduced herself.

"I have a message for you. From the Shadow Guard," she said, lowering her voice. Manco nodded and pulled Brindl off the dance floor toward the outskirts of the pavilion. He walked quickly, his long legs forcing Brindl to double her steps until they reached a quiet table. He held out his hand for the message and Brindl pulled the letter from her apron pocket. He cracked the dark wax seal and began to read, a flash of concern crossing his face. Brindl resisted the urge to peek over his huge shoulder.

"So it is time. . . . Tell them it shall be done," he said, slipping the letter into the pocket of his shirt. "Now would you share some nut punch with me?"

"I would," Brindl said. "Thank you."

"Wait here." A minute later Manco returned with two cups balanced in his hands.

A group of people walked by, clapping Manco on the shoulder for his win. He nodded and thanked them, but the cheerful light in his eyes earlier had been snuffed out by the letter. What could it have said? And what shall be done? Brindl's stomach turned over. What had she gotten herself into? Again, she wondered why the Diosa had chosen her for this task.

"So how did you come to be in this part of Tequende?" Manco asked, once they were alone again.

"I am traveling with the Queen's caravan, as lady's maid to the princess."

Manco's eyes swept over her Earth Guild attire, noting the discrepancy between her words and appearance, but did not comment on it. "The loggers have requested an audience with the Queen."

"And when will she receive you?" Brindl asked, taking a sip of the punch. It was an odd flavor, earthy and bitter, like a liquid version of the roasted nuts her mother used to serve on festival days.

"She will not receive us. We request an audience with her each year, and every time it is denied."

"I see," Brindl said quietly, trying to think of something better to say but failing.

"Never has she made time for us, but here she is at *our* festival to impress rich men from Far Worlds. And still she refuses."

Brindl could not blame him for his ire. She chose her next words carefully. "Not all the Royals are as unsympathetic as she."

"Well, I have met none of them," he said, leaning closer. "Listen, Brindl. If you are working with the Shadow Guard, you know that change is needed in Tequende. The only people Queen Twenty-two will take audience with are her own Moon Guild counselors, inkers all of them, who've never worked an honest day's labor in their lives."

Brindl cringed at Manco's words, and thought of Zarif, his hands so often covered in ink.

"The Earth Guild has been quiet for too long," he continued. "If the Queen won't listen to us, then we shall *make* ourselves heard. With pick and axe, if necessary."

Brindl furrowed her brow in alarm and clasped her knees under the table. "You speak of rebellion? Armed rebellion?"

"Sometimes there is no other way."

"But there is!" she insisted. "Seek audience with Princess Xiomara." Brindl knew she had just greatly overstepped her role as lady's maid, but still she pressed on. "Her interest in each Guild is genuine. She would listen to you. And no one need get hurt."

Manco shrugged. "She is not the one with power."

"Not yet, but she *will* be the next Queen." I hope, Brindl thought, remembering Twenty-two's threat to marry Xiomara off to a Far World prince.

"And while we wait twenty more years for her to be crowned—and I have little faith your princess will be any better than the current Queen—that is twenty years too many. My people will continue to be used for their labor, overworked, undercompensated, and called 'dirts' for their pains. No, Brindl. I will not wait. I will die first before I raise my children in a realm where they are *less* than others due to their name, their birth." Though Manco had not raised his voice, it had become thick with emotion and his hands tightened around his cup.

Brindl sat forward in her chair. "I understand, I do. But

taking up arms against the Queen will prove nothing. How do you expect to stand against the Queen's army, the Second Guard?"

Manco smiled thinly. "Oh, I know the Guard well."

"You're a second-born? You served?"

Manco nodded. "I did, and beyond my four years."

"Did you like it then?" Brindl asked, curious.

"Loved the Guard, hated my centurio," he answered.

"Why was that?"

"Service in the Guard is supposed to wipe out loyalty to your Guild. But dirts . . . we're always dirts, aren't we?"

Brindl looked down at her borrowed Earth Guild tunic and said nothing. The band played a quieter tune now and couples paired off, holding each other closely. Young children mimicked their parents in little twosomes at their knees.

"We were grunts in shiny armor. Well-fed, well-dressed servants trained to kill for our Queen." Manco's voice now sounded bitter. "Do you know how many of the current one hundred centurios are from the Earth Guild?" he asked, pointedly.

Brindl shook her head, but suspected she could guess the answer.

"Exactly none," he answered, then stood up and offered his hand to Brindl.

They parted after that. Brindl tried to enjoy the music,

even took a plate of the beautiful food. But his words played over and again in her mind, stealing the pleasure from each morsel.

Grunts in shiny armor.
Trained to kill for our Queen.
Exactly none.

"It is Brindl come back from the mountains!" Tail said, motioning her to join them on the deck where chairs had been pulled together.

Brindl smiled, cheered to be back among friends after the intense conversation with Manco. For an instant it felt as if she'd stepped into Saavedra's small cottage at the Alcazar. So many evenings they'd spent together, just like this, though Xiomara now sat in the chair that would've been his. How strange to think that despite the distance and divide between them—a farmer, a tradeboater, a miner, a scholar, a princess—Saavedra was their common ingredient.

Tali popped up from her seat and offered Brindl hers. "I'll grab another," she said.

"I've eaten to the point of illness." Chey clutched at his stomach.

"I've never been weak for sweets," Zarif said, "but Nel's pudding could change all that."

"I'm not sure which of the dishes was my favorite,"

Princess Xiomara added, "but how fun to be part of a real Sun Guild family for an evening."

"My family would welcome you any time." Tali pulled her chair into the circle. "And how was your evening, Brin? Did you find your cousin well?"

"Quite well," Brindl said, forcing cheer into her voice. "Recovered and happy with a babe in arms, just five weeks old but so chubby!"

"I do love a fat baby." Princess Xiomara sighed. "They are possibly the best thing on Machué's apron."

"I would respectfully disagree," Zarif said, making a face. "I find babies so . . . unsanitary, perpetually sticky."

The others laughed at his description. Brindl noticed Princess Xiomara was fiddling with something in her hands.

"What is it that you have there, Xia?" Brindl asked, hoping to steer the conversation away from her cousin and imaginary baby. How easy the lies slipped off her tongue!

"It's a carving, a gift from the loggers." Princess Xiomara handed the small object to Brindl, who held it up to the lantern on the table. It was a miniature replica of a Mother's Tree, complete with a tiny house tucked into a hollow.

"It's lovely, but I hope you will see the Mother's Wood in person someday," Brindl said, handing the carving back to Xia carefully. "It is a wonder to behold."

"The Queen received one, too—even grander. The regents took great interest in them."

"Did the loggers not offer one to them as well?" Zarif asked, turning back to his position as royal counselor.

"No." Xiomara shook her head. "Though the regents offered to buy one from them. The loggers refused. Apparently, it is against their code to profit from any part of a Mother's Tree."

"Fascinating," Zarif said, gesturing toward the carving so he might study it. "But why would the loggers not see it as a valuable resource? Clearly they could profit dearly from it."

"Let the questions begin!" Tali said, reaching for ale on the small table in front of her.

"Could we skip questions for just one night?" Chey asked, though he grinned.

Zarif threw his hands in the air. "What is wrong with curiosity?"

"A question for a question!" Tali demanded.

"I can answer your question, Zarif," Brindl chimed in, "if you'd like to know."

Princess Xiomara winked at Brindl. "Well of course he must know."

"It's a godtale I heard just tonight while walking back down the mountain," Brindl continued, "though I doubt I can do it justice."

"Do try." Princess Xiomara placed the little tree on the table, which cast a shadow nearly as magnificent as the carving itself.

"Long, long ago," Brindl began, "Machué's people struggled to find their way after she gave away so many gifts to her greedy children. Daily they suffered, trying to provide for themselves under the hot gaze of Intiq. At night, they could not rest long under Elia before they had to wake and toil again. To make matters worse, Machué's apron began to wear, threadbare from too many crops planted and not enough rain. Long gashes opened in her apron, and even the Magda River went dry. Then, a mighty storm came, but rather than parch the thirst of the land and her people, it swept many to their deaths. The loggers and fisherpeople suffered much. The great wave of water off the mountain washed away their homes.

"But Machué could not bear to see her people suffer, and so she led them up the mountain to a clearing made by the washout. Higher and higher they went, farther than ever before. There they found a great grove of trees, the Mother's Wood, whose astounding size brought all to their knees. They knew this grove of trees was a sacred gift, a sanctuary of the Gods. Machué made them promise never to fell these blessed trees, but to wait until one died a natural death before they would harvest it. Always have they kept this promise and always has there been enough. For Machué provides for her own."

"Praise the Mother," answered Chey in a whisper.

The silence lasted for another moment before the others woke from the spell that Brindl had cast upon them.

Xiomara picked up the little tree again and turned it over in her hands. "Praise the Mother," she repeated.

All palace attire must be impeccably clean and polished.
Never allow your clothes, shoes, or hair to be in disarray.
Wear your white uniform with pride, for it is a symbol of
your service to the Queen.

—CH. N. TASCA, *Palace Etiquette*

SIXTEEN

Intiq arose the next morning shortly after Brindl had fallen asleep, or so it seemed. She stifled a yawn and rubbed her eyes.

"Good morning," said Xiomara, who was already neatly dressed and sitting on her cabin bed. "For all the tossing and turning we did last night, we should have stayed awake and played cards with Chey and Tali."

"True," replied Brindl, exchanging a rueful smile with the princess.

Though they made light of the subject, last night's discovery had been anything but pleasant. As they'd all left the deck and returned to their cabins, Brindl and Xiomara had opened their door and jumped to find a rank, soiled bundle of cloth on the pristine white sheets of Xiomara's bed.

Xiomara's hand flew to cover her nose and mouth. "What in Elia's name *is* that?"

Brindl pulled a handkerchief out of her apron and used it to gingerly pick up the bundle. As the cloth unfurled, they both gasped.

It was Xiomara's nightgown. Only it looked like it had been dragged through the vilest of river mud, and not at all gently. The sleeves were in tatters, the hem nearly shredded. It was as if the delicate nightgown had been desecrated, violated almost.

An icy chill ran through Brindl's spine. "Chey! Tali!" Brindl called, as Xiomara's face paled. The sight and the smell of the gown were horrific, but the meaning behind them even more so.

Someone had been in their cabin.

And someone had left a very ominous message.

After they'd discovered the gown, Tali and Chey had insisted on keeping watch over their cabin door, taking turns throughout the long, sleepless night. Every few hours, Brindl would hear their low voices outside the door as they relieved each other from their post. Though Brindl and Xiomara had both tried to sleep, the rustling from each side of the cabin came in regular intervals as they tossed in their narrow beds.

A knock on the door sounded then, followed by Chey's voice. "May I come in, Princess? I have news."

"Of course," said Xiomara, as Brindl pulled a blanket over her nightclothes.

Chey entered and Brindl felt his embarrassment at being in such close quarters with them. He seemed relieved to see the princess already up and dressed, and she smiled to put him at ease. "What is it, Chey? No more stinky bedclothes, I hope? We had to burn tagua leaves all night just to get rid of the smell."

Chey grinned at her attempt at humor, though Brindl knew he did not take the threat lightly. None of them did. Whoever had left the soiled gown in their cabin had either managed to get past the Queen's guards protecting the caravan or—even worse—didn't have to. Was someone in their traveling party the culprit? The thought raised the hair on Brindl's arms.

"It's good news, or at least Tali and I think so," said Chey. "The Queen is tired of river travel and has no wish to return to Fugaza by boat."

"That *is* good news," replied Xiomara. "The trip upstream will take twice as long, even with the strongest oarsmen pulling us."

Chey nodded. "She's arranging for horses as we speak. We're to ride back to Fugaza on the Queen's Paseo, which should shorten the trip by several days. We leave at noon today."

"I see," said Xiomara. "I guess my cousin has tired of Soga, though I should have liked to stay another day to see the Mother's Wood and meet your cousin, Brindl."

"Another time perhaps. I'll start packing our things," said Brindl, suddenly grateful for their urgent departure. "Why don't you go with Chey and get some breakfast, while I—"

"Sorry, there's one more thing," interrupted Chey. "It's Lord Yonda. He's leaving."

"What do you mean?" asked Xiomara. "Leaving where? Why?"

Chey shook his head. "We were told very little. Only that Yonda's come to some kind of agreement with the Queen and has no further business here. He and his party will ride directly for New Castille. Queen Twenty-two has dispatched some of her guards to accompany them to the border. They leave within the hour."

Xiomara and Brindl exchanged a long look. What agreement could the Queen have made to end the Treaty Talks so abruptly?

"Well, then, I suppose we must say our farewells," said Brindl, knowing that this would be her last chance to glean any new information from the regent.

Xiomara nodded. "Please join us as soon as you're dressed and ready. Your friend Yonda will want to say goodbye to you, I'm sure."

"I'll be right there," said Brindl as they exited the cabin. Something wasn't right about this. She rose briskly from the bed, trying to shake the feeling away, but inside her head the voice kept repeating one word. *Danger.*

"May I have a moment, Lady Brindl?" asked Yonda, taking her by the arm and leading her away from the others. The Castillian riding party had gathered at the edge of town, where fresh horses had been saddled and alpacas loaded with bundles. The Queen had made a short speech in which she bid Lord Yonda safe travels, then she and Lady Ona had quickly departed. Xiomara now circulated among the party, exchanging personal words with each man, servant, and guard. Tali and Chey stayed close by her side, though the princess tried to wave them away several times.

Arm in arm, Brindl and Yonda strolled a few paces down the road, dusty due to the movement of the animals, and Brindl stopped to sneeze. Immediately, Yonda withdrew a handkerchief from his pocket. Embroidered wildflowers edged the crisp white square.

Brindl took it and smiled. "This is much too pretty for a nose, Regent. If it were any bigger, I could wear it to the next ball."

Yonda chuckled. "A pretty nose deserves a pretty kerchief, dear. Keep it. But I have something even prettier for you, and much more useful."

Brindl watched as the Castillian withdrew a small bundle from the inside of his riding jacket. Glancing behind him, as if to make sure no one was watching, he untied the bundle and presented it to Brindl. Inside lay a belted knife holster made of soft brown leather. In one fluid motion, Yonda slid a silver dagger from the sheath, its delicate yet deadly blade glinting in the early light.

"I don't understand," said Brindl, taking a small step backward. "What kind of a gift is this? Are you teasing me?"

Yonda's lips turned up into a smile, yet his eyes remained steely. "I would not tease you, Lady Brindl. Not in matters such as these. The world as you know it is about to change, I fear, and not for the best. I believe you may be in danger from those who see you as a threat."

"A threat? But I don't pose a threat to anyone," Brindl said, still eyeing the dagger in Yonda's hands. "I'm a lady's maid, no more."

Yonda raised his eyebrows. "And a smart one, Brindl. Observant. Thoughtful. Must I tell you that a trusted lady's maid can wield just as much—perhaps even more—influence on royal matters than the highest counselors, the most-decorated commanders?"

Brindl's thoughts raced. Was he speaking about *her* or Lady Ona? What was he trying to say?

Yonda's eyes did not leave her as he slid the dagger back into the holster. "It would put an old man at ease if you would wear this at all times, my dear. Strap it to your leg, so it cannot be seen. Trust no one, even those closest to you. And should you ever need my help, you must not hesitate to ask."

Brindl stood still, unsure of how to reply. Finally, she reached out her hands and took the holster. "Thank you. I'll do as you say, though I hope never to have need for it."

"As do I, my dear. Now I believe we must part ways before the riding party leaves without me."

"Forgive me, Lord Yonda, but may I ask why you're going so soon?" Brindl tucked the dagger into the deep pockets of her dress. "I thought you would return to Fugaza with the rest of us."

Yonda gave her another long look, then smiled again. "I've done all I can do for the present, and I've no wish to antagonize your Queen and Lord Paulin any longer. I've secured what I need. My way back to New Castille will be shorter from here, saving me a week's journey. I'm an old man and miss the comforts of my wife and home."

"Of course," said Brindl. "I wish you a safe and fast journey, then. My sincere regards to Lady Yonda and your children, my lord." Brindl gave a small curtsy and dipped her head.

Yonda took her hands in his. "I shall miss your company, Lady Brindl. May your Tequendian gods protect you."

———

It had been a long day in the saddle, and Brindl was sore though the ride had given her many quiet hours to puzzle over the nightgown, and to replay her conversations with Manco and Yonda. She turned them this way and that, trying to piece together any hint she might've missed. Occasionally, she would look up to offer an apologetic smile at the travelers they passed, who scurried down the ditches to make way for their entourage.

An hour before sunset, the Queen's party stopped for refreshment to let the servants go ahead with the carts to set up camp for the evening. They dismounted their horses alongside the Paseo to stretch weary legs and admire the view. The landscape of east Tequende looked to Brindl like the staircase of the Gods. The farmers had carved lush green terraces into the foothills to rotate their crops among the curved steps.

"How ingenious," Paulin had noted, then peppered Zarif with questions concerning crop yields and profits until the group made ready to leave.

They mounted their horses again and had traversed the Paseo for less than a league before they were halted by a dray, which had broken down in the middle of the road. A rear wheel had obviously come off its axle, spilling a full load of syrup from the looks of it. The barrels had tumbled all over the path, oozing their tarlike liquid everywhere. The driver, who had his hands full trying to unharness his mules from the dray, looked at them in apology.

The Queen was not pleased. "How far is it to our camp?" she asked one of her guards, who had dismounted to assess the situation.

"Just a few minutes' ride, Your Majesty, once this cart's out of the way."

Zarif rode up to get a closer look. "Is that cordillo tree sap?" he asked the driver, who nodded warily. "I thought so. That will ruin our horses' hooves for certain. We'd have to reshoe them. Best we go around, Your Majesty."

The Queen frowned. "Through the ditch?"

"Unless you'd prefer to wait, though from the looks of it, that could be hours."

The Queen turned her frown to the cart driver, whose eyes flew to the ground. "Very well," she said, then led her horse off the road.

A moment later her curses could be heard through all Tequende.

The ditch, it turned out, had been flooded by a faulty irrigation stream, converting it into a knee-high trench of mud. As the horses picked their way through, they kicked up muck everywhere, covering the party head to toe in dark brown splatters.

Brindl, whose horse had balked at the commotion, fell behind with the Queen's rear guard, who muttered curses as colorful as the Queen's. A big clot of mud had just landed on his cheek.

Brindl tried not to laugh. "I do hope there's a good bathhouse at the campground," she joked, as he ran a sleeve over his face.

"And a laundryhouse as well," he said, looking meaningfully at Brindl's white Moon Guild attire now turned to brown. "First the Queen's nightdress, now this. Servants will be busy tonight."

Brindl snapped her eyes open. "The Queen's nightdress? What of it?"

The guard shrugged. "Somehow got dropped in the mud. Twenty-two was furious last night. Almost dismissed every last servant."

Brindl looked back at the dray, whose driver now stood by his mules, watching their retreat. Then she looked over at the irrigation stream, where someone had diverted its course into the ditch by digging a little furrow through the ground. The cause for all the discord. There was so much mess, all the mud and . . . dirt.

Everyone was covered in *dirt.*

"I see," said Brindl.

" 'I've secured what I need,' " whispered Xiomara. "What do you suppose Yonda meant by that?"

Brindl shook her head, the candlelight casting shadows

on the tent curtains behind her. After cleaning themselves up, the Queen's riding party had gone straight to bed, exhausted by the day's long ride. A small tent had been assembled for Brindl and the princess to share, and Brindl was finally able to fill her in on the earlier conversation with Yonda.

"Maybe he simply meant that he secured some kind of trade agreement," Brindl replied, turning in her camp bed. "What else could he mean? Though it does seem as if Lord Paulin has gained the majority of the Queen's favor . . . if not all of it."

"They do seem taken with each other," Xiomara agreed, "though my cousin isn't the type to be won over by a pretty face. She already has a hundred handsome men in Fugaza vying to be her consort."

"Yes, but none of them wields the power that Paulin does," Brindl replied, remembering her conversation with Yonda. "He's the chosen regent of the Queen of Andoria. That makes him the most important man in the Nigh World right now."

"True. So perhaps their growing *alliance* is a good thing for Tequende?" asked Xiomara, though her voice betrayed her doubt.

"Possibly . . ." Brindl chewed on her lip. *But that's a lie. Their alliance will not bring justice to the Earth Guild. And the Shadow Guard will fight back. The nightgowns, the muddy ditch. Those were warnings.*

"What is it, Brin?"

Brindl opened her eyes in surprise at the use of her shortened name. Xiomara, always so formal, now almost felt like a sister. They had been through much since leaving Fugaza. And Xiomara was in danger. Brindl owed her the truth.

Even if she had to break another oath to do so.

"There's something I need to tell you, Xia."

A lady's maid must never offer her own opinion unless directly requested to do so by a Royal. If a Royal has previously stated her own opinion on the matter, defer to that opinion.

—Ch. N. Tasca, *Palace Etiquette*

SEVENTEEN

week later, Brindl stood at the back of the Queen's receiving room with Zarif. Twenty-two's throne, placed on a dais, elevated her at least a foot higher than the tallest person in their assembly, Maita Khuno, chief paymaster of the Sun Guild. He was a slim man with pointed features, who obviously liked clothes and wore them well. Brindl found the fashions of most Sun Guilders jarring and garish, but his were understated with a few colorful flairs. A woven belt clasped by a copper sun around his sleek tunic reminded Brindl that he was a native of Porto Sol, center of the Sun Guild's trade and commerce.

Paulin sat by the Queen's side, though his chair was

placed on a lower tier, slightly behind her. In the far shadows behind them both stood Lady Ona, no doubt observing the assembled crowd with her usual scrutiny. Brindl had not seen any of them since their return to Fugaza.

"Surely we should tell the Queen?" Xiomara had said that night in the tent, after Brindl had told her about the Shadow Guard.

Brindl shook her head. "We can't, Xia. She'll see them as a threat."

"But *aren't* they?"

"No, not if we can convince the Queen to treat with them. And if she sees them as rebels she won't. She needs to see them as *her* people—as loggers, quarrymen, miners—just as they want to be heard by *their* Queen."

"But what if she won't listen?" asked Xiomara. "Then what?"

Brindl took a deep breath. "Then we go find the Diosa."

The two had not spoken of the matter since, but Brindl knew it was not far from either of their minds. Xiomara had requested an audience with Twenty-two several times since their return, but had been denied. Nor had Xiomara been invited to any counsel meetings until now.

The assembled crowd had remained quiet, standing along the perimeter of the room once they had knelt before the Queen. Twenty-two now summoned Maita Khuno and Jaden before her. The two men strode forth and stood at attention.

"I've asked you here today for historic reasons," Twenty-two began, clasping her hands in front of her. "Lord Paulin, on behalf of Oest Andoria and his sovereign Queen, Beatríz of Andoria, has proposed a trade agreement between our two realms, which I have accepted. It will mean great changes for Tequende, but I expect you will embrace them as I have, and fulfill your duty as leaders of this realm."

This will not be good news, Brindl realized. Though she could not see their faces, she knew that Jaden and Paymaster Khuno must have felt the same, for their bodies both tensed before the Queen.

"At sunrise tomorrow, the Second Guard will take control of the pearlstone quarry, the gold mine, and the Mother's Wood on behalf of the Crown. All quarry workers, miners, and loggers will begin round-the-clock shifts to increase production. Jaden, you will install Second Guard centurios and guards at each location to oversee all operations and ensure compliance."

"Your Majesty—" Jaden began, but the Queen put up a hand to silence him.

"Paymaster, you are to instruct your Sun Guild merchants that they will no longer be trading in these three commodities. All pearlstone, gold, and Mother's Wood now belong to the Crown for commerce with Andoria."

"But, Your Majesty, please, this goes against all prior agreements!" exclaimed Maita, his gloved hands raised in distress. "The guilds have worked in harmony for centuries with careful allegiance to each guild's warrants and labors. The Sun Guild has always been responsible for trade and commerce, both within Tequende and with our neighboring realms. Surely you don't mean to strip us of our Gods-given right to the realm's most valuable commodities?"

"Those commodities belong to Tequende, of which I am sovereign," replied Twenty-two, her face hardening. "The guilds swear an Oath to *me* above all else."

"The Oath of Guilds promises every second-born child of the realm to your service. Is that not enough, Your Highness? You would now take our livelihood as well?"

The room became deathly still as the Queen narrowed her eyes at Maita. "You will notify the Sun Guild of this new arrangement, Paymaster, or I will send my guards to do it for you."

Maita stood perfectly still as the color drained from his face. "Yes, Your Majesty," he finally said, looking down at his boots.

Jaden stepped forward, his eyes flashing. "As Commander of the Second Guard and your sworn Sword, I beseech you to reconsider, my Queen. The Guard serves to protect Tequende's borders from *foreign* dangers," he said, his eyes flickering to Lord Paulin, "not to oversee Earth Guild operations. Like the Sun Guild traders, I'm afraid the Earth Guilders will not take kindly to us meddling in their labors, especially if we mean to work them like slaves. They will protest."

"They will *not*," said Twenty-two, "if they value their lives and families."

An audible gasp now sounded from several people in the room. A small smile played across Paulin's lips, as if he were enjoying a theater performance.

"But, cousin," cried Xiomara, approaching the throne, "will this not feel like punishment to our people? The miners sacrificed many lives in the Battle for the Alcazar not six moons ago. And think of the Sun Guild traders who set their boats aflame on Lake Chibcha to come to the aid of the realm—"

"Enough! I have sufficiently reimbursed them for their losses," interrupted the Queen. "As we came together to defeat Telendor's mercenaries, so shall we come together now to turn Tequende into one of the greatest powers in the world. The alliance between Tequende and Andoria will make us the richest realm in the Nigh World. It's a small sacrifice I demand of the guilds to bring glory to Tequende, and ensure none will ever dare again usurp the royal family."

"Your Majesty," Brindl said, stepping forward. "Perhaps you are unaware, but the Mother's Wood is sacred to the loggers. They only cut down the trees that are diseased, and even then, the wood is never sold, but only used to honor Machué. Anything else would be sacrilege. I assure you, they will not cut the Mother's Wood for commerce." She glanced at Paulin, who looked bored by her words.

"Oh but they will," replied the Queen. "My guards will ensure it. As for you, Lady Brindl, do not presume to advise me. Your ties to the Earth Guild cloud your judgment. If you again speak out of turn, you will be dismissed as Xiomara's lady's maid and returned to your pigeonkeep duties."

Brindl nodded, though ached to speak her mind and be dismissed from this miserable company. How could Twenty-two do such a thing? The fate of thousands of people rested on the decisions of this one woman, a woman who surrounded herself with advisors who did nothing but agree with every word she said. Brindl remembered Saavedra then, the wisest man she'd ever known, who had been dismissed by this same Queen for telling her what she didn't want to hear. How Brindl wished she could return to the mines again, back among people who were honorable and hardworking, who treated others with respect.

"Is there anyone else here who intends to defy me?" asked the Queen, her cold eyes traveling around the room.

Brindl stole a glance at the assembled party. Most every-one looked at the floor now, all but Xiomara and Jaden, neither of whom flinched from Twenty-two's glare, though they did not speak.

"A wise choice," continued the Queen, "for I will not be questioned. Any man or woman, of any position or guild, who refuses to carry out my orders will be immediately pun-ished as a traitor to the realm. Do I make myself clear?"

Brindl swallowed the lump in her throat, and managed to say, "Yes, Your Majesty," in unison with the others. She knew as well as everyone else in the room the punishment for treason.

Death.

A lady's maid must never be seen in untoward company that would compromise her status or propriety. Indeed, a lady's maid represents the Royal for whom she serves, so her appearance is just as important—if not more so—than the work she provides. She must never appear mussed, breathless, sweaty, or stained, even in private.

—CH. N. TASCA, *Palace Etiquette*

EIGHTEEN

f course you can go, Brin," said Xiomara, motioning for Brindl to sit down. "I'd go with you myself, only I think I've made the Queen mad enough for today, and my absence from the palace might be seen as an act of treason."

The Queen's threats from earlier that day still rang in their ears, and Brindl had done little but stew over them. Then Lili had slipped her a message from Tonio, and she'd had to feign a headache so she could lie down and decide what to do.

"Meet me at the Fray tonight," the note had read.

As if I can just come and go as I please, thought Brindl.

She'd spent the next hour formulating a dozen lies in order to excuse herself from the palace for the evening, but in the end she couldn't bring herself to say them. Xiomara was her friend now. And she knew about the Shadow Guard . . . at least in theory. But Brindl had named no names to her, and she would not give away Tonio. If she couldn't tell Xia the *entire* truth, she would at least tell her some of it.

"It's just that it's been weeks since I've seen Tonio—you remember me telling you about him, the cake maker's son?" Brindl said, her words rushing out like a stream. "And Lili's brother-in-law, Moth they call him, will be fighting tonight at the Fray, and I *did* promise Lili I'd go and see him some-time. I'll come back as soon as—"

"Brin, it's fine, you don't need to explain. Besides, you haven't had an evening to yourself since you saw your cousin in Soga."

Brindl's stomach clenched, loathing the previous deceit she'd wrapped herself in. One day, she would explain every-thing to Xiomara. But right now, she couldn't.

"Go," Xiomara said, lightly tapping Brindl on the knee. "To be honest, it may be the last pleasant evening there if my cousin insists on operating the quarry night and day from now on."

Brindl nodded. "True." She wondered how the quarry workers would take the news tomorrow when Jaden showed up to announce the Queen's mandate. Not well, she thought, shuddering. She did not envy Jaden his task tomorrow.

"Take Tali with you," Xiomara continued, "but don't say a word to her about tomorrow's announcement. She knows something is brewing, but Jaden wishes to keep quiet until he's had another chance to speak with the Queen. I'm still hoping he may be able to talk her out of it. So not even a peep, Brin. You know what a hothead Tali can be when given orders she doesn't agree with," she added, trying to earn a smile from Brindl.

Brindl's mind raced. She couldn't take Tali with her. How would she talk with Tonio? "But—"

"I insist," said Xiomara, rising from her chair. "Tali needs a good distraction as much as you do, and from the way you've described the Fray—grown adults beating each other to a pulp—she'll love it. Now I'd better change for dinner, but I expect to hear all about it when you return."

"I have to admit, these Earth Guild clothes *are* very comfortable," Tali said, as they bumped down the dirt road to the quarry in the back of a hay wagon. "I could get used to this."

Brindl grinned at her friend, who had borrowed an earth-colored tunic, matching trousers, and a pair of worn but sturdy work boots from the night cook's daughter. Brindl had changed into some of her old clothes as well so they could blend in with the crowd. The last thing she wanted to do was draw attention to herself at the Fray by arriving in a lady's maid gown with a Second Guard warrior at her side. And the Gods only knew how Tonio would respond if he found out that Brindl had brought a guard to their meeting. She still wasn't sure how she'd manage to speak to him without Tali around.

"This is incredible," Tali said, as the wagon pulled to a stop and the passengers piled out in Quarry Town.

"Yes it is," Brindl agreed and looked around in appreciation. Once again, she felt immediately transported, far away from her real life and responsibilities. Standing among the bright, slim cottages that perched over the giant pearlstone pit, she felt like part of a whimsytale. From the gleam in Tali's eyes, Brindl knew that she, too, was enchanted by the cheerful buildings surrounding the quarry like a tumble of children's blocks.

A current of excitement ran through the crowd as Brindl and Tali followed the others down the ramp into the great torchlit quarry. The pearlstone walls glowed orange and red, almost as if the pit itself were on fire. Brindl scanned the crowd for Tonio, but either he wasn't there, or he purposefully kept himself at a distance.

"How about here?" Brindl said, choosing seats close to where she and Tonio had sat at the last Fray.

"Perfect," said Tali. "Right in front of the ring. So where is this mysterious cake-making boy anyway? And does he know you're betrothed to the princess's counselor? I wonder which of the two is more jealous?" She gave Brindl a wink and a light elbow to the ribs.

"Stop it," said Brindl, elbowing Tali back. "I'm sure neither of them cares one way or the other. Tonio and I are just friends, and Zarif—"

At Brindl's hesitation, Tali turned and tilted her head. "And Zarif what?"

Just then, a woman came by with a donation basket and the girls paused to throw in several coins.

"Zarif's too preoccupied to think of me," Brindl finally said. "Being *forced* to marry is the exact opposite of romantic, I'll have you know."

Tali grimaced. "I can't imagine how awkward that must be for both of you. As for him being too busy to think of you, that I *can* imagine, only too well."

Brindl glanced at her friend, then took her hand. "One day, perhaps, Jaden's service to the realm will not require so much of him."

Tali shrugged, then squeezed Brindl's hand in return. "I'm afraid that day will be a long time coming. Meanwhile, I live vicariously through Nel's letters. She has at least a dozen suitors in every port, poor girl. Everyone falls in love with the pretty girl who can't hear or speak, but cooks like a goddess. She's going to whack them all with a ladle one of these days."

Brindl laughed. "I think our Chey was quite smitten with her, too, was he not?"

"And she with him, for he actually made an attempt to learn our sign language to communicate with her. But Nel's busy learning our father's trade now, and Chey is steadfast in his devotion to the Guard . . . and the princess." Tali leaned closer to Brindl and lowered her voice. "Ever since Xia's nightgown was found that night . . . well, he refuses to be more than a hammer's throw away from her. Sometimes she has to order him to his quarters so that he can get some rest, otherwise he'll spend night and day at her door."

"I've noticed. Chey is loyal as a packhound, that much is sure."

"Look, it's starting!" Tali said, pointing to the ring.

The same announcer as last time, gray of hair but large in size, raised his arms to quiet the crowd. "Due to a quarry injury earlier today, which left Axe with a crushed hand, his match with Iron Skull has been postponed until the next Half-Moon Fray. That takes us right to the main fight of the evening, the battle for victory between two of Quarry Town's renowned rivals and biggest bruisers: Pretty Boy versus Moth!"

The crowd roared as the two fighters entered the ring from opposite sides of the quarry. Pretty Boy took center stage immediately, throwing his arms wide and clapping them over his head. The audience began to clap with him while he strutted around the ring, showing off his handsome physique and a thick mane of hair dyed the color of mountain berries. Meanwhile, Moth stood off to the side with his arms crossed over his massive, shirtless chest, his bald head gleaming in the torchlight. He almost looks like a statue, thought Brindl, though a slight smile played on his lips as Pretty Boy danced around him. The two reminded her of a fancy bird trying to catch the attention of a bored mate.

The horn sounded and the fight began. Moth rolled his shoulders back, threw his head from side to side, then came in quick to land the first two blows to Pretty Boy's ribs. Pretty Boy spun on his feet, recovered from the onslaught, then kicked a heel square into his opponent's gut. The crowd gasped, but Moth didn't flinch. Instead, he drove straight for Pretty Boy again, aiming his fists for the rib cage, attacking the same spots he'd hit before.

Pretty Boy grimaced, his playfulness for the audience now over. He circled around Moth, taunting him with words. Though Brindl couldn't hear everything, she heard enough to know that Pretty Boy was now making rude comments about Moth's wife. The ploy worked. Furious, Moth dropped his arms and charged like a bull. Pretty Boy, anticipating the move, dove underneath him and grabbed both ankles. Moth fell hard, but reached for Pretty Boy as he did so, forcing them both to the ground. The men began to grapple, elbows and knees flying as they tried to pin each other for the win.

"This is amazing!" Tali exclaimed, her eyes riveted to the scene in front of her. "It feels so good to see some real fighting instead of waiting around for our invisible enemy."

"It *is* exciting," Brindl admitted. "Although kind of horrifying at the same time."

"Moth is clearly stronger but he's slow to turn, have you noticed?"

Brindl shook her head and shrugged. "I see nothing but a pile of arms and legs."

The figures were back on their feet now, wearing each other down with strikes, kicks, and jabs. After a few minutes, Pretty Boy, for all of his initial bravado, seemed fatigued, the methodical beating of Moth taking its toll. While Moth had also slowed, his strength appeared undiminished, his accuracy relentless.

Tali had balled her hands into fists and was now yelling as loudly as anyone in the crowd, warning Pretty Boy to keep his arms up. Pretty Boy jumped unexpectedly, cracking Moth's knee with a sweep kick. "Gods, how I miss sparring at the Alcazar," Tali said with a sigh.

Brindl shook her head. "You were black-and-blue for nearly a year, Tali."

"It's a mind game as well as a physical one. It's exhilarating in a strange way."

"Very strange," agreed Brindl.

"Oh!" they both cried in unison as Moth flipped Pretty Boy to the ground like a sack of sand, then quickly pinned him with his knees.

The horn blew.

"Moth wins!" the announcer called.

The crowd went wild as Moth pumped his fists in the air. Pretty Boy limped out of the ring, lifting a feeble hand to acknowledge the audience, who cheered him off the stage despite his loss. He'd fought hard and the crowd was appreciative. Brindl laughed as Tali stuck her fingers in her mouth to let out a loud whistle. After a few minutes, Moth signaled for the crowd to quiet.

"We only had one fight tonight, but you were promised two," he called. "Who here is brave enough to fight me now? Who here is man enough to best me?"

Before Brindl could react, Tali jumped to her feet. "I am!" she yelled, standing on her seat. "I'll fight you!"

The crowd began to laugh then, as if Tali had told a joke. Moth shook his head. "Little girls aren't allowed to fight in the quarry. But you are brave, I'll grant you that."

"Let me fight!" yelled Tali. "Or are you scared this little girl will grind you to quarry dust?"

The crowd erupted in hoots and whistles.

Machué have mercy, Brindl thought, trying to tug Tali back down to her seat. But it was no use. Tali was heated now, and wouldn't budge.

Moth grinned, his white teeth gleaming. Brindl wondered how it was possible he still had teeth left after the fight. Some young people seated above them began to chant "Let her fight! Let her fight!" As Brindl turned to look at them, she caught a glimpse of Tonio sitting nearby, watching her and Tali with interest. He raised his eyebrows at her but did not smile.

"It seems the people would like to see what you can do," Moth called up to Tali, his voice booming inside the pit. "What is your name, girl?"

"I am Tali," she hollered back.

"Tali who? You're not from Quarry Town."

Brindl stiffened and clutched Tali's wrist. *Now what?*

Tali glanced at her with a twinkle in her eye. "*Princess Tali of the Royal Bone Breakers,*" she yelled, as the crowd roared in approval.

Moth's grin now took over his whole face. "Then do come down, Your Royal Highness, and welcome to Quarry Town," he said, sweeping an arm out in front of him and bowing low.

Tali kicked off her boots and ran down to the ring. "Blow the horn!" she cried to the announcer, and they were off.

Moth, amused by Tali's gumption, watched her skip around him for a while, his arms barely raised in defense. He has no idea what's coming, Brindl thought, smiling to herself right as Tali dashed in with a scissor kick to his chin. Moth reeled back in surprise as the crowd hooted. Tali kept up the quick movements, spinning around the large man like a sundial. Moth tried to grab her a few times—Brindl knew that if he managed to latch on to an ankle, elbow, anything, and throw her to the floor, the match would be over—but Tali continued to evade him easily with her small size and fast speed.

Finally, Moth connected a walloping blow to her shoulder, forcing her backward, but Tali somersaulted away from him, escaping his grasp. The crowd continued to cheer wildly, even more entranced by this fight than the last. Spurred by their enthusiasm, Tali pivoted around Moth and jumped him from behind. Wrapping her legs around his waist and her arms around his neck, she clung to him like a tribella vine, choking him for all she was worth. As Moth stumbled, trying to pry Tali's arms from around his neck, Brindl felt her heart beat double-time inside her chest. If the giant man fell to the ground now—purposefully or not—he would break Tali's bones.

Finally, Moth stomped his foot twice, signaling defeat.

Tali slid from his back and fell to her knees, weakened by the exertion. When she lifted her head, Moth glared at her from above, his face hard as pearlstone. Then his face cracked into a wide smile and in one sweeping motion he lifted Tali straight onto his shoulders.

The crowd jumped to their feet, erupting in cheers. "Honor over strength!" they chanted as Tali beamed from her high perch atop Moth.

Brindl let out a long, slow sigh and wondered if she'd been holding her breath for the entire fight. Thank the Gods Tali hadn't suffer any serious injuries. Still, she'd have some bruises to explain tomorrow.

"So who is she really?" a voice whispered into her ear.

Brindl jumped in surprise. "Tonio!"

"She fights much too well for a kitchen maid. She's your guard friend, isn't she?"

Brindl shrugged, trying to seem unconcerned. "It was the only way I could leave the palace. You didn't give me another choice."

"Did you deliver the message to Manco?"

"Yes."

"And his reply?"

" 'Tell them it shall be done,' he said, though I can't say I agree with it," Brindl added, remembering the shredded nightgowns and muddy detour around the Paseo.

Tonio opened his mouth to say something and then stopped. "And what news of the regents?" he finally asked.

Brindl hesitated. "The Queen has made a trade alliance with the Andorians. I believe an announcement will be made tomorrow."

"What kind of trade?"

Brindl shook her head. She would not be the one to deliver the news. "I don't know the details. But one thing I do know, Tonio, is you must tell Moth and the Shadow Guard not to defy the Queen's orders. She will not see reason. You will be punished."

"If enough people make her *see* reason, perhaps she will."

"Don't be foolish, Tonio, she has an army behind her."

Tonio's eyes darkened and turned back to the pit in front of them, where Tali sat on Moth's shoulders, laughing and waving as they strode through the cheering crowd. Musicians strolled after them like a parade, playing a cheerful jig. Several villagers began to dance.

Brindl's heart sank.

Everything would change tomorrow. There would be no more laughter in the quarry pit. No more music, no more dancing, no more Fray Fights.

Tomorrow, her friend Tali, tonight's hero, would become the enemy in Quarry Town.

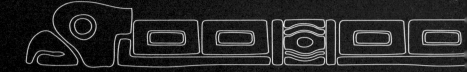

A lady's maid should never involve herself in official matters of the realm. When such topics are discussed by the Queen and her counselors, it can help to pretend you are deaf or that they are speaking a foreign tongue. Concentrate on your posture instead.

—Ch. N. Tasca, *Palace Etiquette*

NINETEEN

our Majesty, I beg you to reconsider,"
said Jaden, kneeling before the Queen's
throne. Once again, Brindl stood in the
back of the room, though the assembled party was much smaller than
yesterday's. Jaden and Xiomara had
requested a private meeting this time, without counselors,
without guards, without Lord Paulin. Only Lady Ona stood
in the shadows behind the Queen. Xiomara stood next to
Jaden.

"As commander of the Second Guard, as your chosen
Queen's Sword," Jaden continued, "I must warn you of
the damage this trade agreement will do to the realm. Our
wounds from the Alcazar are still fresh. This alliance with

the Andorians comes too quickly on the heels of their complicity in that betrayal."

The Queen smirked as though highly amused, though Brindl saw fire in her eyes. "*That betrayal*, Commander? You mean the one perpetrated by your own father?"

Jaden's jaw hardened. "My father died for his treason, as was just. But why should we give the Andorians amnesty for their role? Instead you mean to reward them with Tequende's greatest riches."

"Your father hired mercenaries. Paid soldiers. That they came from Oest Andoria is of no consequence," the Queen said, her voice rising in anger. "Those men, those snakes, did not act on behalf of their Queen or regent. They drew their swords for your father's riches, for the gold he stole from *me*, his Queen."

Jaden clenched his fists and turned his head away.

Xiomara stepped forward. "Cousin, we have no more claim to that gold than Telendor did. By rights it belongs to the Earth Guilders. As does the pearlstone and Mother's Wood. I must agree with Jaden. I fear this trade agreement with Andoria will not sit well with our people. We must be fair to them. We must listen."

Queen Twenty-two rose to her feet, her body rigid with fury. Brindl resisted the urge to take a step backward.

"Listen to the weak? Take a look around you, cousin.

The Far World has taken over every last realm in the Nigh World save Tequende. Why do you think that is?"

Xiomara remained rigid, though Brindl could see her heart pounding in her chest.

"Why?!" the Queen yelled.

"Because the Far World had superior strength, weapons . . ." Xiomara began.

"Because they are stronger. Because the Nigh World is weak!" The Queen laughed then, though there was no mirth behind it. "The Nigh World is over, do you understand, cousin? For Tequende to survive, we must adapt to Far World ways, take our lessons from them. Or did that old fool Saavedra delude you into believing that Tequende was different, that we could resist?"

At the mention of Saavedra's name, Xiomara stood straighter, her shoulders resolute. "Saavedra was right. We can resist. We should resist. We are not Andoria. We are not Castille. We are Tequende. We are the children of Machué, the Mother of us all."

"Enough! Ona, summon Centurio Larus at once," the Queen demanded, then turned her icy gaze back to Jaden and Xiomara. "It was a mistake to grant you this audience, I see that now. I've allowed you both too many intimacies, too much confidence in your own authority. I shall not make the same mistake again."

The doors opened and Centurio Larus strode in. He's been waiting outside this whole time, Brindl realized. The muscled, silver-haired warrior dropped to one knee before the Queen. "At your service, Your Majesty."

"Arise," she ordered the hulking man, then turned to Jaden. "Give him your sword."

Jaden shook his head, incredulous. "My Queen—"

"Give him your sword!" the Queen shouted, pointing her finger at Larus.

Jaden let out a slow, measured breath, then drew his sword, the revered Blade of Tequende, from its sheath and offered the hilt to Larus.

The centurio took the blade with a smug half smile, then bowed at the Queen. "You honor me."

"Gather every palace guard and ready them to ride for the quarry," the Queen said.

"Yes, Your Majesty. We will await you at the palace gates."

"No," she said, looking at Xiomara with a sly expression on her face. "I think not. I no longer wish to ride to the quarry. I've decided it shall be my cousin, the Queen-in-Waiting, who will announce the new trade agreement to the quarry workers. It will be instructive for her to assert herself as future sovereign of Tequende, will it not?"

Xiomara paled. "Please, I cannot. Please—"

"Do not beg like a dog. You are a future Queen. Learn to act like one."

Brindl wanted to race forward, to stand next to Xiomara's side in the face of this monster, the Queen. How could she do this?

"As for *you*," the Queen continued, turning back to Jaden. "You have one day."

"One day, Your Majesty? I don't understand."

"One day to say good-bye to your realm. At sunrise tomorrow you will be escorted to the border. Your service to Tequende is no longer required."

Brindl stifled a gasp.

Only Jaden remained still. "You would exile me for offering honest counsel?" he finally said, his voice low and quiet.

"I would. Though there is another alternative if you prefer it," the Queen said crisply. "Shall I have Larus sharpen his blade?"

The room grew silent.

The gray sky cast a leaden sheen over Quarry Town, making even the brightly painted buildings look washed-out and tired. As the palace guards, mounted three abreast, had made their way to the quarry, the Sun God, who had begun the day with a brilliant warmth, had suddenly fled the sky. Even Intiq does not wish to bear witness to the coming announcement, Brindl thought, wishing she could flee with him.

Word of their arrival had preceded them, of course, and it seemed that every last inhabitant of Quarry Town now filed into the quarry pit like ants. Brindl fought to control her pounding heart as the procession neared. Princess Xiomara had insisted on riding in the lead, with Centurio Larus on her right. Zarif, bearing the Queen's flag, accompanied her on the left. Brindl rode directly behind them, flanked by Tali and Chey. One hundred palace guards followed, uniformed and armed.

We look like we're marching to war, Brindl thought, her stomach turning somersaults. Perhaps we are.

She glanced at Tali in concern then, not for the first time that morning. Though her friend had not said a word during the ride, Brindl knew that Tali would be reeling from the news of Jaden's exile. Even Chey remained quiet and brooding, his tan brow creased in worry. *And they still know nothing of the coming announcement.*

In fact, of their entire cavalcade, only four of them knew what was about to happen at the quarry—or at least what was about to be announced. After they had been dismissed from the Queen's receiving room, Xiomara and Brindl had gone immediately to apprise Zarif of the situation, who had been waiting on tenterhooks for their news. "Clearly she means to punish you, to make you their scapegoat, Xiomara," he'd said, shaking his head. "Though I see no way you can refuse."

Even when her life had been threatened, Xiomara had remained strong, collected. But Zarif's words had brought tears to her eyes. She rose from her chair. "I can't go through with it. I'd rather leave here with Jaden than inflict something so cruel onto our people."

"Don't say that," Zarif had said, placing his hands on her shoulders. "One day you'll be Queen and you will right these wrongs. Your time will come. But for now, you must do as the Queen says. If she threatened her own Queen's Sword with death, I fear she'll have no compulsion to be lenient with whomever else gets in her way . . . even her own cousin. I'm sorry, Xia," he added softly, as she sank back into her chair.

Brindl had said nothing during the exchange, but a dozen thoughts rattled inside her like caged birds trying to free themselves. How would the quarry workers respond to the announcement? What would the Shadow Guard do? Would this be all they needed to take up arms and fight back? Though she longed to flee underground and find the Diosa, to beg for help, there was no way she would abandon Xia. Not now.

The procession came to a stop at the top of the quarry, the mounted guards forming a semicircle on either side of Xiomara and her attendants. Brindl looked down into the pit, where every man, woman, and child of Quarry Town stood assembled along the ramps, draping the vast canyon like ribbons. Moth and five other men—Brindl recognized

Goat and Axe among them—strode forward to the middle of the quarry. The quarry foremen, she gathered.

Xiomara dismounted, signaling everyone else to stay on horseback.

When Moth bent his knee in deference, the entire quarry followed suit, each head bowed to the marbled ground.

"Good citizens of Quarry Town," Xiomara called, her voice loud and strong, though Brindl saw her hand tremble slightly as Zarif passed her the scroll. "I come bearing an announcement from Queen Twenty-two," she continued, her words echoing off the pearlstone walls. "Please rise."

Moth was slow to his feet, Brindl noticed, but every last person in the quarry waited until he had risen before doing the same. She glanced at Zarif. Though his facial expression had not changed, she saw comprehension in his eyes. Moth held great power here. His response to the announcement would be crucial. The quarry workers would take their lead from him.

Xiomara unrolled the parchment and began to read. The announcement wasted no words. "'Effective immediately, the quarry shall operate without cease, rendering all pearlstone to the Queen for trade with our allies. A Second Guard patrol will be assigned to the quarry to monitor all operations and oversee compliance. Any man or woman who defies this mandate will be charged with treason and punished accordingly.'"

A startled murmur ran through the crowd. Brindl heard Tali swear under her breath beside her. Almost as if he heard it, too, Moth's eyes now landed upon Tali.

Brindl felt Tali go rigid next to her. Gods help us, she prayed, fighting the urge to grab Tali's arm, lest she race down to the pit again. She should never have let Tali fight last night. "Shhhhh, say nothing, Tali. Now is not the time," she whispered.

Moth, whose eyes had not left Tali, finally nodded to himself, as if he had just come to some kind of understanding. "Is this the new order of Tequende, then?" he called out, stepping forward. "The Queen steals our livelihood while the Guard steals our dignity?"

"No!" cried Xiomara and Tali at the same time.

Xiomara looked at Tali in alarm, who had quickly dismounted from her horse and approached the lip of the quarry.

The crowd, many of whom now pointed at Tali in recognition, began to boo and hiss, their discontent erupting through the pit like a pot of boiling water.

Centurio Larus dismounted as well then, eyes flashing and hand on his hilt, as if he were about to take off someone's head.

"Xiomara, let me speak," Tali begged. "There's been a misunder—"

"Stand down!" the princess ordered, glaring first at Tali, then at Larus. The two guards hesitated, then did as they were told, each taking a step backward. Brindl could feel Tali struggling for control below her. Zarif glanced quickly at Chey, who placed a firm hand on Tali's shoulder.

Xiomara raised her arms to quiet the crowd, though a ripple of angry murmurs continued until Moth raised his own hand. Xiomara cleared her throat. "I entreat you, *all* of you," she said, her eyes leaving Moth to scan the quarry, "to obey the Queen's orders, to make this sacrifice for our realm, to keep peace in Tequende for the glory of the Gods."

"You would invoke the Gods in this matter?" Moth called. "Are the Gods to feed us then? How are we to eat if you take away our only source of earning?"

Xiomara blanched. Brindl closed her eyes. Why had they not thought of this question earlier? So stupid of us, she thought, stealing another glance at Zarif. She could see the remorse in his eyes and knew he felt the same. *We didn't think of it because we never have to worry where our next meal comes, those of us shut away in the comforts of the palace.*

Xiomara stood straight and raised her arms again. "On my solemn word as Queen-in-Waiting, you will be fed in exchange for your labors," she replied with confidence, though Brindl saw the worry in her face. The princess now spoke with no authority on the matter, no permission from the Queen to make such promises. Brindl had a feeling this would not go well later.

The crowd hushed completely then, waiting for Moth to speak. Once again he took his time, his steely gaze pivoting back and forth between Xiomara and Tali. Not once did he lock eyes with Centurio Larus, as if the man's presence meant nothing to him.

"Please," Xiomara said, extending her arms to the crowd. "Please."

She is begging, Brindl thought. The Queen will not like this.

"For Tequende!" Centurio Larus yelled, raising an angry fist as his words echoed along the pearlstone.

The crowd did not return the rally cry. Instead, silence fell like a hammer.

Moth turned his back and walked away.

Larus stepped forward as if to charge the man, but Princess Xiomara stayed him with one gesture, raising her hand.

Then, the entire crowd followed suit, turning their backs to the princess as Moth had. In every direction, the dark hair and plain dress of an entire village quietly filed out of the quarry. Only the scuffle of feet and the echo of a babe in arms gave any indication of so many thousands nearby.

Brindl shivered, as if caught in the air before a violent storm, pregnant with destruction.

No matter your position in the palace, never misunderstand your first loyalty. Everyone—from the highest counselor to the lowest kitchen maid—serves the Queen foremost, no one else. All actions, words, and service should be guided by this simple principle.

—CH. N. TASCA, *Palace Etiquette*

TWENTY

he Queen sat on her throne, again. Brindl noticed that she was reverting to this place of power more often of late. Perhaps she meant to intimidate others from her dais. It forced those speaking to her to look up. Princess Xiomara looked diminutive next to Centurio Larus and withered in front of the Queen's escalating rage.

"My Queen." Larus kneeled and rose at the foot of the dais. Jaden had never made such displays of humility, unless it was part of a formal ceremony. The Queen obviously enjoyed her new Sword's formality, a satisfied mask painted on her face. Xiomara curtsied as custom required but did not speak.

"Did you announce my plans to the quarry workers?

We shall commence the new schedule at dawn." The Queen motioned to a nearby servant who brought a tray of sweets to her. She plucked one from the colorful array but did not eat it, placing it next to her steaming cup of tea.

"It was announced, as you required," Xiomara said, with a slight pause. "It was not well received."

The Queen waved her hand as if swatting an invisible pest. "No matter," she said, then turned her gaze on Centurio Larus. "I trust you took care of any dissent."

"I would have arrested their leader and whipped him right then," Larus said, glancing at Princess Xiomara, "but she did not allow it."

"Because it was unnecessary," Princess Xiomara said quickly. "The man didn't threaten me, only turned to leave."

"He turned his back on your words," Centurio Larus corrected, looking at the princess with clear disdain.

"You do not mean to say he turned his back on her while she spoke?" the Queen asked, her voice incredulous.

"Not only him, but the entire crowd," Larus reported, obviously pleased to be bringing his version to the Queen. "They *all* turned their backs on her." He paused then, and pressed his lips together. "Which means they turned their backs on *you*, Your Majesty."

Twenty-two shot out of her throne. The small table next to her wobbled and crashed to the pearlstone floor, the delicate plate and cup shattering. The servants, who normally would have raced to retrieve the mess, did not move. The Queen clenched her hands, then released them, her cheeks red with anger.

"They dare turn their backs on the royal family?"

"They dare worry how to feed their children, how they will survive," Xiomara said, her voice even, as if she had not just witnessed the outburst of the Queen.

"We are done here. Larus . . ." The Queen turned her gaze back to the centurio. "Seize the quarry at dawn. Use force if necessary. Deal with traitors who disrespect my orders immediately."

"You do not mean to strike down your own people?" Xiomara asked.

"They are not *my* people if they disobey me!" the Queen hissed, her eyes narrowing. "They are traitors, deserving death, no better than Telendor. We will not bear such weakness again. Ever."

"Still, all Tequendians deserve a trial if accused of treason. As it has always been . . ."

So it shall always be, Brindl thought, though she did not say the words aloud. Invoking the sacred response would only infuriate the Queen more.

"Get out of my sight!" the Queen yelled, throwing her arm across the assembly before her. "Attend to business of your own."

At a slight nod from Xiomara, Brindl wasted no time scurrying from the throne room and directly to the bakery. She had to warn Tonio and the Shadow Guard. She only hoped her words could convince them to stand down tomorrow. Otherwise, blood would certainly spill in the quarry. Brindl skipped down the steps to the last level of the palace, then raced out the door to the outer building.

Turning the corner toward the bakery, Brindl barely avoided a collision with a girl carrying a basket of loaves. Finally, she opened the bakery door and was relieved to see Tonio, his hands deep in a trencher of dough, his face animated as he spoke to another baker across from him. Brindl hesitated for one moment longer. She hoped it wasn't the last time she'd ever see him happy.

As Brindl approached Tonio, the bustling of the great bakery hushed, people standing poised to complete their tasks, heads turning in abject curiosity. Brindl inhaled deeply, hoping to keep the color off her cheeks, her distress carved in the lines around her forehead, her mouth. Tonio spotted her last of all, and his eyes widened.

"I must speak with you," Brindl said, wasting no time.

"Can we meet at the top of the bells?" Tonio asked, turning the dough once more in his hands. This small action caused everyone to resume their task and the chatter sparked once more, like the notes of a small band finding its tune.

"I'm afraid not," Brindl said. "It's quite urgent."

With a nod, Tonio pulled his hands from the dough, wiping them on the splattered apron he wore over his clothes, then headed toward the corridor. Brindl realized he was moving toward the enclave where he kept his pearlstone sculptures. For several minutes she followed him into the darkness, the air becoming cooler and damp but still smelling vaguely of cake.

"Burnt bread! I forgot the key. Should I turn back?" Tonio asked, turning to face Brindl.

"There's no time, and I have much to tell you."

Quickly, Brindl told him about the earlier encounter at the quarry and the Queen's response to it.

"So the Queen means to seize all the pearlstone from the very people who mine it?" Tonio said, shaking his head.

"It's worse than that. You must warn the Shadow Guard. . . . Get word to Moth."

"Why? Has he been discovered?"

"He defied Centurio Larus today, who would have retaliated, but Xiomara stopped him. She won't be able to do so again. The Queen has authorized military force tomorrow, and Larus will not be afraid to use it. You must tell Moth to stand down."

"No one tells Moth to stand down. But I'll warn him of the Queen's orders. He'll decide best how to respond."

"Then hurry! There's no time to lose. I worry not only for him, but for all the quarry families, truth be told."

"I'll go straightaway. Will you tell my mother I won't return until late?"

"Yes! Go."

Tonio squeezed Brindl's hands. "Thank you, Brindl. You did the right thing by telling us."

Then he was gone, racing through the corridor and out of sight. Brindl pressed herself against the rough, cold stone. At least she had managed to do this one thing. She turned to go back to the bakery and noticed the toe of a slipper peeping out from a dark corner. A Moon Guild slipper.

Lady Ona stepped out from the darkness.

"Why, Lady Ona, what brings you to these dark halls?" Brindl tried to keep her voice light, a casual greeting.

"I think you know, traitor," replied Lady Ona, stepping into the corridor.

Black tunnels.

"I'm no traitor. But I am an Earth Guilder, concerned for her people."

"You wear the gown of a Moon Guilder now, or have you forgotten?" Lady Ona's lip snagged at one corner, as if she smelled something putrid.

Brindl looked down at her white gown. She often forgot she was wearing it these days. But she was no more Moon Guilder than a bird with a cat's tail was a cat.

"I was just trying to help. People, even *children*, could get hurt tomorrow," Brindl said, trying to reason with Lady Ona.

"You have no right to interfere with the Queen's commands."

"I'm not interfering with her commands. I'm merely informing those who might suffer from them." Brindl sounded more confident than she felt.

"Stand aside," Lady Ona demanded, "in the name of Queen Twenty-two!"

Brindl had not realized until then that she had blocked Ona's path, but now she deliberately widened her stance, hands on her hips. "I don't *work* for Twenty-two," Brindl said, "I work for Twenty-*three*."

Lady Ona slapped Brindl across the face, then bolted down the hallway.

Brindl, bewildered, placed a hand on her cheek. Though her face stung, the punishment to come would be worse. Surely Ona would go straight to the Queen with Brindl's treason. Still, she had to tell Mama Rossi about Tonio's sudden disappearance. She owed him that.

If the bakery staff had stared at her before, they were enthralled now. They must think Tonio slapped me, Brindl realized. She found Mama Rossi in her own quarters, looking out the window.

"Mama Rossi?"

"Oh my! What happened to your face, Brindl?"

"It's no matter."

"Of course it is! Who would do this to you?" Mama

Rossi bustled to a cupboard to grab a rag. She dipped it in a large bowl of water and wrung it out in her hands, then placed it on Brindl's stinging cheek.

"Truly, Mama Rossi, I need to be brief."

"What is it? Why is Tonio not with you? Tell me he did not do this. . . ."

"No, no. Of course not."

"A small mercy. Still, I cannot—"

Brindl interrupted. "Mama Rossi, Tonio has gone to speak with Moth at the quarry. He'll be back as soon as he can."

"Who is Moth?" Mama Rossi asked, and Brindl knew then that his mother had no inclinations of her son's activities outside the bakery.

"A friend. A friend in trouble. What matters is that Tonio needed to go to the quarry to warn him."

"Warn him of what?"

"I'm sorry, Mama Rossi, I've no time to explain." Brindl handed the rag back to the woman and turned to go.

"But, my Tonio . . . he will be safe?"

"I pray to the Gods it is so."

"These are not comforting words for a mother."

"I'm sorry. I promised him I would get word to you, but now I must go."

Brindl walked back to the palace as fast as she could without drawing attention to herself. As she bustled up the stairwells toward the rooftop aviary, she put a hand over her face to hide the mark so no one would stop to ask her about it. She'd paused long enough in a hallway mirror to see the telltale signs of splayed fingers and palm tattooed on her pale face. Just as she reached the top of the last stairwell to the roof, two guards grabbed her.

"We've been waiting for you."

"Unhand me!" Brindl said, trying to maintain her composure.

"We take no orders from traitors!" the smaller one said, pinching her tightly under the arm, making her wince in pain.

"Where are you taking me?"

They practically dragged her across the roof, her white slippers barely touching the ground. She feared they would force her back down the stairs to the dungeons, but instead they headed toward her old tower. They opened the door and pushed her inside. Brindl hit a wall and slid down it, crumpling on the cold floor.

She heard a bolt slide outside the door.

Second-born servants shall have no leave from the palace until their service is complete, six years hence. Anyone caught leaving the palace grounds without explicit permission from a Royal—via the chamberlain—shall be subject to the harshest punishments and ramifications thereof.

—CH. N. TASCA, *Palace Etiquette*

TWENTY-ONE

Brindl paced her small room like a blue-jacket with clipped wings. She thought about each scene that had brought her to this terrible place. *Have I made things worse with all my meddling?*

The rest of the day passed in agonizing beats of her heart as a hundred questions raced through her mind. Had Tonio been able to spread the warning before it was too late? Could the people of Quarry Town protect themselves, if not their property tomorrow?

Brindl looked out the narrow window to the aviary. What had happened to Lili and Farra? Were the birds being taken care of?

As night fell, she tried to sleep, but her thoughts would

give her no rest. She finally gave up and continued her pacing until she heard a noise at the door. She stepped back as the outer bolt slid open.

"Tali!" Brindl rushed to her friend and they quickly embraced. "How did you get here? Are there no guards posted outside?"

"Not anymore. Larus has them all summoned to ready them for tomorrow."

Brindl shivered despite herself. "So the Queen will go through with this."

Tali paused. "And worse."

"Worse? What is it, Tali? Tell me!"

Tali placed a hand on Brindl's shoulder and gently pushed her into a chair. "The Queen has ordered a public execution in the quarry tomorrow. To remind others what happens to traitors."

Brindl could barely get the word out of her mouth. "Who?"

"Moth." Tali knelt down and took Brindl's hands in hers. "And your friend Tonio."

Brindl's breath caught in her throat and she stifled a sob. "This is my fault. I was trying to warn them. Instead I gave them away."

Tali squeezed her hands. "There's more, Brin. Zarif and Chey . . ."

"Dear Gods. Tell me they are safe?"

"For now, yes. But they've embarked on a dangerous task. Xiomara sent them after Jaden." Tali's voice shook, her face betraying her feelings for the ousted commander. "The Queen's soldiers plan to kill him before he ever reaches the border."

"The Queen ordered this?" For a second an old godtale flashed through Brindl's mind, about a woman so bewitched by riches the Gods turned her into pearlstone.

Tali nodded, and Brindl watched her face transform from fear to anger. "A guardsman loyal to Jaden overheard the plan and told Xiomara. I would have gone myself, but Zarif and Chey insisted I stay here. Someone needs to look after Xiomara, and I can stay in her chambers with her." Tali closed her eyes, then stood. "In fact, I must get back to her now. I don't like to leave her alone."

Brindl rose from the chair. "Wait, I'm going, too," she said, reaching under the bed for her old Earth Guild clothes.

"Going where?"

"To the Diosa." Brindl pulled on the soft leather boots of her former life. She hadn't realized how much she'd missed them until she slid them on.

"You're the Queen's prisoner, Brindl. You risk your life if they catch you escaping."

"Then I will risk it. But I won't sit here while they kill

Tonio tomorrow. You know I can't." Brindl buckled the belt around her tunic. "My hair," she said suddenly.

"What of it?" Tali asked, confused.

"Too fancy." She pulled the pins out with impatient fingers.

"Have you any shears?" Tali asked.

Brindl shook her head but ran to a drawer and pulled out Lord Yonda's parting gift to her. She had almost forgotten about it until now. "Here," she said, handing the dagger to Tali and strapping the leg holster underneath her tunic.

Tali paused, then hacked off Brindl's long tresses to chin-length. "There," she said, pulling back to examine her work. "With a little soot on your face you'll look just like a char girl from the kitchens."

"Thank you, my friend," Brindl said quietly, as Tali rubbed ashes on her cheek.

"Not that long ago, I was the prisoner and you had the key," Tali said, with a small, sad smile.

"May the Mother protect you."

"May she protect us all."

Brindl pushed through the bakery doors and followed a dim light flickering from the family quarters. Of course Tonio's mother would be awake. How could she sleep? Mama Rossi sat at the table, a full cup of coffee in front of her, an untouched biscuit on her plate. Her eyes looked like they were focused across a wide sea.

"Mama Rossi?"

The woman looked up, her face etched with worry. She stared at Brindl in confusion until recognition finally dawned.

"You? Why are you here? And dressed like those you betray."

Brindl opened her mouth, then closed it again. Mama Rossi appeared to have aged a decade or more. The pleasant play of a smile on her lips was long gone, as if it had never been there. Her hair, usually tidy, lay in tangles against her scalp. How vulnerable she looks, Brindl thought. I did this to her.

"It's your fault Tonio is inside this mess!" Mama Rossi said, rising from the table. She waved a hand from side to side as if trying to shoo away a pest. "This Shadow Guard"—she paused, trying to find the words—"you brought this . . . this nonsense to my son."

"That's not true," Brindl said, defending herself. "Tonio introduced the Shadow Guard to *me*." She reached out a hand to place on Mama Rossi's arm, but Tonio's mother stepped backward and shook her head.

"That couldn't be. He wouldn't be involved with those people. Tonio's always been such a good, honest boy. What did you do?"

"He still is a good, honest boy, Mama Rossi," Brindl said, her voice softening. "He was only trying to improve the lives of Earth Guilders in Tequende."

"With treason?"

"That may be what the Queen calls it, but most anyone else would not."

"Does anyone else matter if he loses his life tomorrow?" Mama Rossi said, a sob escaping her lips.

"That's what I'm trying to prevent, but I must get to the Diosa before it's too late. Will you help me? I don't know how to get to the salt mines from here."

"You know the Diosa?"

"No. But she knows me."

"Can she save my Tonio?"

"I don't know," Brindl answered truthfully. "But I mean to ask."

Mama Rossi grabbed her shawl and threw it around her shoulders, suddenly full of resolve and vigor. "Come."

Brindl followed Mama Rossi down the stairs and through the dark corridors where Tonio had once shown her his secret sculptures. They turned down several hallways and descended more steps before they finally came to a heavy stone door. Mama Rossi pulled on the forged handle but could not budge it. Brindl added her strength until it opened at last.

The stairs leading down to the mines were narrow and damp, but a series of torches lit the way.

Mama Rossi grabbed Brindl and pulled her into a fierce hug. "You must save him, Brindl. You must." The woman's voice caught then and she could say no more, her eyes wet with tears.

"I will do everything I can."

"Machué bless you then, child."

Brindl moved as nimbly as she could on the slippery steps into the darkness. Her eyes adjusted quickly, accustomed to the dim light from years of teaching first-year salters in the mines. The torches illuminated her path, the spaces between their arcs a place to gain speed in the flickering light. Most people would be frightened to delve into the crust under Machué's great apron, but it felt like coming home to Brindl. Her pulse slowed and breathing steadied with each step.

The cave walls were a deep orange rather than the pale sand of home in Zipa, but the rich loamy smell of things being born and dying, the bumpy texture of stone beneath her hand, all felt the same. Brindl closed her eyes, and felt peace, unequivocal peace, for the first time in months.

Time was impossible to measure inside the tunnels. Brindl knew only that hunger pulled on her twice, and her legs wobbled after hours of following the signs to the Diosa's cave. The paths were clearly marked above each tunnel where crossways intersected, and when she passed the symbol for Zipa, a candle for the Festival of Light, her heart ached with the desire to follow it. But she turned to the tunnel marked with the Diosa's own symbol, a single eye, and smartened her pace.

She passed few people and knew it must still be nighttime above the earth, for the miners had not started working yet. *Though that will change soon, if the Queen gets her way,* Brindl thought, shaking her head in dismay. *Round-the-clock production. As if the miners don't work hard enough already.*

Finally, she found herself at the entrance of the Diosa's cave. The largest man she'd ever seen stood sentry at the covered entrance.

"Brindl Tacora of the Zipa Salt Miners, late of the Fugaza palace," he intoned, with a slight bow.

How did he know?

"The Diosa is expecting you."

The Queen must never be defied, for she has been blessed by the Gods. Charged by Machué to care for her children, educated by the light of Elia, and made wealthy by the coin of Intiq, she is the sole divine presence in Tequende, and godly in her own right.

—Ch. N. Tasca, *Palace Etiquette*

TWENTY-TWO

rindl pushed aside the tapestried curtains and walked into the chamber. On her left, life-sized statues of the three Gods stood in a row. Intiq, Elia, and the simple yet beautiful Machué were revealed in their human forms, crafted from the finest salt and glowing despite the darkness. Brindl knelt before the Mother, who held a miner's pick in one hand, a hoe in the other, and touched her bare feet, worn smooth from all those who came before to give homage. As she stood, she kept her eyes on the floor rather than look to the sculptures of the Gods on her right, depicted in their divine form, an act of humility for her Guild.

As she left the chamber, another room vaulted and arched above her, like one of the Far World cathedrals drawn in

Saavedra's books. At first Brindl thought another statue of Mother Machué had been placed at the back of the chamber, this one seated on a throne of salt and painted in vines and flowers.

But it was the Diosa waiting for her.

"Come, daughter. Tell me your needs."

Brindl stepped forward slowly, her head bowed with reverence, and knelt before the woman.

"Arise, daughter of Machué. You have done all I asked of you."

Brindl stood and looked into the face of the Diosa, ageless and pale, though her arms and legs were adorned with tattooed vines and flowers in a riot of vibrant colors.

"Have I?" Brindl asked. "Forgive me, but I'm not sure I ever understood what you asked of me. Or why."

"When danger nears, let Brindl be your eyes and ears," the Diosa said solemnly, though her eyes gleamed.

"Yes, but you asked me to be the eyes and ears of opposing forces—the realm and the Shadow Guard."

"Not the realm. Not opposing forces."

"But Princess Xiomara . . ."

". . . is not the realm."

Brindl lowered her eyes. "Nor an opposing force. She knows about the Shadow Guard. I broke my oath of silence to Machué."

"That is why I chose you."

"Because I would break my oath?"

"Because you would know when the truth became more important. Not all oaths are made equal, daughter."

"But I've only made things worse," Brindl cried, falling to her knees again. "My friends are in trouble. The Queen means to execute Moth and Tonio tomorrow. Please, you have to help them!"

The Diosa paused, then placed her hand on top of Brindl's head like a mother to a small child. "What would you have me do, daughter?"

"Come back with me! Come with me to Quarry Town!"

The Diosa did not speak for a full minute but seemed to travel into herself, closing her eyes, lifting her chin. Brindl waited. Was she praying? Was she looking into the future that some said she could see?

"I have never left these mines," the Diosa finally said, gazing at the walls around her. Her voice sounded much older now, ancient even. "If I leave, I shall not return. The world above is not my providence."

Brindl's heart sank.

"But it is *your* world, Brindl. Command me and I shall go."

"But you are the Diosa! I cannot *command* you," Brindl said, her voice trembling.

"Brindl Tacora, listen to the voice inside you. It's the Mother's voice, and it has never failed you, has it?"

Brindl shook her head.

"Is it time?" continued the Diosa.

Yes, the voice said. *Yes.*

"You must go with me," Brindl said, "and we must go now."

The Diosa nodded, then held up a hand.

A small boy appeared from a dark corner.

"Ory!" Brindl cried, as the boy rushed into her arms. The two hugged tightly, like siblings kept apart after a loss.

"The packhounds are ready, Diosa," Ory said, pulling back from Brindl's arms though he did not release her hand.

The Diosa rose from her throne. "Then we are ready, too."

"Perhaps you two should wait here," Brindl said to the Diosa and Ory as they emerged into daylight from a mountain cave, just outside the perimeter of Quarry Town. The wooded area would offer them some protection until Brindl could assess the situation.

"We will not," the Diosa answered, waving away Brindl's words with her hand. The Diosa was now dressed as a quarrywoman, though Brindl had not seen her change during the journey. It was as if she had summoned the clothes from thin air, the soft gray dress covering the colorful tattoos on her arms and legs. If it weren't for the bright orange fabric wrapped around her head, Brindl would not have known her from the other women of the quarry.

As they headed to town, an unpleasant sound began to drift toward them. The sound of a town under attack. The panicked cries of women and children echoed off the pearlstone. A cloud of smoke wafted across the overcast sky and choked the air. Ory took the Diosa's hand.

"Is that fire?" Brindl asked in alarm.

The three hurried around the last bend to find Quarry Town in chaos. Residents poured out of their dwellings, some carrying children, others helping the elderly, as flames licked out the windows of the stacked quarry homes. The brightly colored facades of the houses disintegrated, folding in on themselves and collapsing in heaps. Bits of fabric and wood floated through the air amid the sparks, oddly reminding Brindl of the Festival of Light in Zipa. Only this was no festival.

Shocked and horrified, Brindl felt her feet anchored to the ground as she witnessed the scene. Women trying to corral their children away from the destruction. Babes crying in the arms of whomever held them. Men, young and old, shouting instructions to each other, hammer and picks in hand, running toward the quarry. *What in Tequende is happening here? Have the Andorians come again?*

Brindl recognized a few faces from the night of the Fray. One musician held his small stringed instrument in his arms as if it were a child, tender and protective. The old announcer who looked so confident and commanding when speaking to the audience, appeared confused and lost.

"Ory, lead these people to the mines!" Brindl called, as she began moving through the crowd. A little girl wailed in the middle of the street, separated from her family in the throng. Brindl scooped her up and handed her into the arms of the old announcer. "Go with that boy," she yelled, pointing to Ory. "All of you! He'll lead you to safety!"

"To me, to me!" Ory yelled, waving the crowd toward him.

"You go with them," she said, turning to the Diosa, but the priestess of Machué had disappeared in the madness. Brindl fought down a wave of panic and searched for the orange head cloth in the crowd, but to no avail.

The pearlstone walkways danced with the colors of the fire, reflecting the destruction of an entire village. Dense smoke filled Brindl's nose and throat and she gasped for air.

"This is what traitors deserve!" Centurio Larus yelled from atop a horse. He held a lit torch in his hand and waved it among the frightened people. "This is what happens when you harbor criminals!"

No, Brindl thought. No!

Larus rode through the crowd, followed by his Second Guard legion. This couldn't be happening! The Guard had turned on its own people!

"Everyone to the quarry!" Larus shouted. "Go!"

The mounted guards began herding people down into the quarry pit, as if cattle to the slaughter. Brindl looked in every direction, but there was no escape. They were surrounded. She only hoped Ory and the Diosa had managed to return to the mines with as many people as possible. She filed down into the quarry with the frightened crowd, the smell of their sweat and fear mingling with the acrid cloud of smoke.

As Brindl made her way down the winding ramp, her mind flashed back to the Battle for the Alcazar. The awkward positions of the dead on the ground. The blood-splattered stones by the lake. The strangled cries of those in pain. She shook the images out of her mind, lest the horror return here.

Finally, they reached the floor of the quarry, and the crowd quieted. Perhaps it was calming to do something so ordinary, to gather in the quarry as if for a fighting match or their everyday work of cutting pearlstone.

One by one, heads turned to the north face of the quarry, their eyes riveted upward, their mouths open. Brindl followed their gaze.

There, at the top of the precipice, was Queen Twenty-two herself, her face a mixture of rage and revenge.

During the Time of Queens, there has never been any civil strife in Tequende, for each man, woman, and child knows his or her place in society. While other realms face domestic unrest, even war, Tequende enjoys peace, prosperity, and proliferation of the arts, due to our strong sense of duty and unconditional loyalty to the Queen. Because our realm is so pristine, changes of any type should simply be avoided. For what is the point in change when all is near perfect as it stands? Therefore, saddle yourself to your duties with gratitude and know that you make an immeasurable difference no matter how small the task may seem.

—Ch. N. Tasca, *Palace Etiquette*

TWENTY-THREE

The crowd didn't dare move as Queen Twenty-two, escorted by Centurio Larus, made her way down to the quarry. Lady Ona and Lord Paulin came behind her, then Princess Xiomara and Tali. Brindl could not make out the faces of her friends, but knew the distress they would be in. The party made their way to a raised platform on the quarry floor, no doubt where the pit foremen would normally supervise pearlstone operations.

The Quarry Town citizens shuffled together for comfort and solace. Men put protective arms around the shoulders of their wives and children. Women rocked babes in arms and pulled older tots closer. It was as if the entire crowd held its breath to see what new cruelty might be in store.

Meanwhile, the Queen's soldiers made a circle around the perimeter of the quarry floor, hands on weapons, waiting for orders. Brindl could not believe how much this felt like a siege, like they were surrounded by enemies instead of their own monarch, their own Guard! Carefully, quietly, she pushed forward to the front of the crowd. She didn't know what was happening, but she needed to be with Xiomara and Tali, come what may.

The Queen stepped forward and raised her arms. "Residents of Quarry Town," she began, the irony of her words a bitter blow, as their town lay smoldering above them. "Before anyone gets hurt, I must have your cooperation."

Cooperation? thought Brindl. Before anyone gets hurt? How could the Queen look at this crowd and consider hurting them any more? She had just burned down their homes.

A young tot to Brindl's left started crying then, gaining volume with each wail. The father holding her tried to soothe her, but she could not be quieted. An elderly woman reached for the babe and the large man handed her over. The old woman pressed her cheek to the child's, one face withered and wrinkled by years of hard work, the other smooth and golden in the light. The woman began to hum a lullaby in the girl's ear and she hushed at the sound of the familiar tune.

"Listen to your Queen!" Centurio Larus bellowed, his voice echoing through the pearlstone walls.

"I want the leaders of this *Shadow* Guard to reveal

themselves *now*," the Queen said, "or every person here shall be guilty of treason and suffer accordingly."

Moth was the first to step forward, the crowd parting for him instantly, though several people murmured their dismay.

"I am the sole leader of the Shadow Guard," Moth called up to the platform. "The rest here are innocents," he said, motioning to the villagers. "Let them be!"

"Silence!" the Queen demanded. "I know there is another in this crowd. My patience grows thin."

"Here I am," a familiar voice called as Brindl's heart caught in her throat. Tonio threaded his way through the crowd to stand beside Moth.

"Guards, execute these traitors immediately!" Beside her, Larus signaled and two guardsmen on either side of the platform raised their bows.

A collective gasp followed her directive. The crowd pushed back from Moth and Tonio, who now stood alone in front of the raised dais.

"No!" cried a woman near Brindl, two sobbing children under her arms. Moth's head whipped around, making eye contact with her, his face registering helplessness for the first time. His wife, Brindl thought. His children.

The guards pulled their bows and nocked an arrow in each one, their deadly points trained on the two men in front of them.

Brindl rushed forward. "Don't fire!" She stood in front of Moth and Tonio with arms outstretched, desperately trying to make her small frame as large as possible.

Behind her Moth whispered in a rough voice, "Don't. They'll kill you, too." Tonio did not speak but put a hand on her shoulder.

All eyes turned to the Queen for her response.

"Little peasant. Bird girl. I'm glad to see you here." Though the Queen smiled, her voice spat venom. "I believe we have you to thank for leading us to these traitors. And now you can die along with them."

Brindl's legs shook and her body felt dipped in icy water. But she held her stance.

"Then do it! Kill me. I'd rather die than live under your reign, where you would enslave your people for your own profit! Where you would burn a village to prove a point!"

Brindl closed her eyes and waited for death. Her mind rushed back to her childhood in Zipa, pushing cart after cart of salt into the white sun after hours spent under Machué's apron. Her mother's eyes, the warm embrace of her father, the silly grin of her brother. Then to the Alcazar, bent over a book as Saavedra patiently taught her to unlock the world through reading. Zarif and Chey and Tali, their faces flashed in her mind's eye. Ory, Boulder, Lili, Pip. Xiomara. And just as she braced for the arrow that would kill her, she felt someone take her left hand. Then someone else took her right.

Tali and Xiomara had jumped down from the platform and now stood on either side of her, blocking the archers from Moth and Tonio.

The crowd froze. Surely the Queen would not fire on the princess, her own *cousin*?

The Queen locked eyes with Xiomara, who stood taller and lifted her chin. Brindl squeezed her hand, her heart nearly bursting with love for her friend, with grief as well. For the Queen now looked undone, like a child's doll whose stuffing poked through the loose seams. Lord Paulin leaned over and whispered in her ear. Lady Ona looked on with a smug smile. *They have no use for a princess who would defy them.*

The Queen stepped forward, her white slippers smudged with the dirt of the quarry, the hem of her gown frayed and stained. She pointed to Centurio Larus. "Execute them all! They are traitors to Tequende."

"In the name of the Mother, stand down!" a voice demanded. The crowd slowly parted and the Diosa appeared in their midst. She had shed the quarrywoman's dress and headscarf, and she now appeared as Brindl had first seen her—like a priestess of the Earth, an otherworldly apparition. Though she wore the simple tunic of an Earth Guilder, the tattooed vines and flowers on her bare arms and legs seemed to come alive, as if they were growing, blooming somehow. Her pale hair gleamed like spun silk, her eyes like emerald gems.

When she reached the platform, she turned and raised her arms above her head. "My people. I am the last living Diosa, daughter of Machué."

Brindl dropped to her knees, her body moving of its own accord. Xiomara and Tali, still holding hands on either side of her, followed suit, as did Moth and Tonio behind them. One by one, every last person in the quarry fell to their knees, save those on the platform and the guards on the perimeter, though Brindl noticed several soldiers exchanging troubled glances. *The Earth Guilders among them. Their allegiance will be tested now.*

"What is this hoax? Who are you?" cried Twenty-two above them. "The Diosa is a whimsytale, nothing more."

The Diosa turned toward Twenty-two and raised a palm to her. Miraculously, the Queen froze, whether shocked by the Diosa's defiance or put under some kind of spell, Brindl couldn't truly say.

The Diosa turned back to the crowd before her. "Ten moons ago I had a vision that when the puma, hound, and condor united, the monster in our realm would be defeated. You have witnessed the monster today, but look upon the future of Tequende now."

The priestess walked over to Tali and exchanged a warm

look with her. She took Tali's hands in hers and stood her before the crowd. "I give you the puma, fierce and courageous!" Next she helped Brindl to her feet. "Look upon the hound, loyal and wise!" Finally, she stepped over to Xiomara, but instead of taking her hands, she placed her own upon the princess's head, as if conferring a blessing. "Behold the condor, honorable and majestic, the *true* and rightful Queen of Tequende, in the name of all the Gods!"

The moment seemed suspended in time, floating between never and forever. Rising to their feet, the crowd erupted in cheers and chants, their faces washed of fear and replaced by hope.

"Praise Machué, Mother who guides us!"

"All hail Queen Twenty-three!"

Brindl knew that history was written in such moments. Though she stood side by side with her friends, she felt as if she were watching the scene from afar. She glanced up at the platform, where Twenty-two still stood like one of the statues in her palace. Then Centurio Larus pushed his way forward, crossbow in hands.

"There is only one Queen," he bellowed.

He aimed the crossbow at the Diosa.

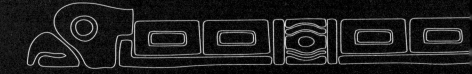

When the Queen reaches the age of fifty harvests,
she steps down from the throne and passes it on to the
Queen-in-Waiting. The ceremony of cessation takes place
on the Queen's name day and the realm entire celebrates the
sacrifice she has made, and the fruits of her life's labor.

—Ch. N. Tasca, *Palace Etiquette*

TWENTY-FOUR

oth moved in a single leap, pulling the Diosa into his arms, rolling his giant frame around hers in a cage of safety. But Larus's arrow found a mark in Moth's thick neck, killing him instantly.

"Avenge your leader, your friend!" the Diosa cried, rising from his motionless form, her arms spread defiantly.

At her words, the crowd snapped out of their trance and sprang into action as if they had practiced. The elderly gathered children like chicks to take them to cover among the piles of pearlstone. Men and women scrambled to hiding spots, pulling out weapons from hidden caches. The picks, hammers, and axes, though crude in comparison to the swords and crossbows of the guards, looked menacing in the hands of a people now fueled by determination and anger.

The guards, startled at first, began to tighten their circle, trapping the villagers in the middle.

Tali drew her sword and charged up the side of the pit with a willing group of quarrymen following. They quickly sliced a path through the ring of soldiers and gained the advantage on one side, climbing above their opponent with the ease of people whose hands knew pearlstone like the faces of those they loved.

Brindl and Xiomara rushed to a small wooden catapult that had been uncovered and struggled to ready it. Although Brindl had never operated one herself, she had seen them used during the Battle for the Alcazar. As Princess Xiomara placed apple-sized pearlstones into the contraption, Brindl released them into the oncoming soldiers as fast as she could. Several hit their marks, while others crashed into the quarry walls, adding to the din below.

The guards continued to circle, their superior weapons and training giving them the advantage. Centurio Larus's entire legion of one hundred palace guards had been called to service, and they fought with precision.

Brindl watched as Goat, Pretty Boy, Axe, and others tried to engage individual soldiers in battle, to break their noose around the quarry, but the guardsmen gave no quarter. They continued circling, dodging blows, their swords poised and menacing.

"Kill any who stand in your way!" Larus cried, aiming his crossbow into the pit and firing it into the crowd. A scream filled the air as a young man, no more than thirteen harvests, fell to the ground, an arrow through his chest. A woman, his mother certainly, ran out into the madness and crumpled to his side, weeping.

Brindl, furious, turned to Larus. "You would kill a child in cold blood?" she shouted, then turned to the approaching soldiers. "Is this what the Second Guard has become? Burning homes, murdering *children*?"

Centurio Larus aimed his crossbow at Brindl and nocked an arrow. But at the last second he changed targets and loosed it at the Diosa. The priestess dropped instantly, an arrow through her heart.

The crowd stilled then, the fighting halted, as everyone stood in shock. The Diosa, their spiritual leader, was dead. Moth, too. The young boy. . . . Who would be next?

"Surrender!" Larus yelled. "The quarry is mine!"

The villagers looked at each other in despair, some of them lowering their weapons. Fallen bodies littered the quarry, like dolls thrown from the hands of an angry god. Blood stained the white pearlstone.

Just then a large soldier stepped out of rank and ripped off his Second Guard jacket. "This quarry is *not* yours," he yelled, throwing the uniform at Larus's feet. "I fight for the Diosa, for Tequende, not you!"

At his words, a dozen more guards followed suit, ripping off their jackets and joining the villagers in the pit.

"For Tequende!" they yelled, as the heartened quarry-men took up the fight again.

Brindl's knees wobbled, but she bent again, pulling back the catapult's leather apparatus and releasing the stone.

Slowly, methodically, the tide of the battle turned as the quarry fighters rallied with the help of the guards who now fought by their side. The remaining guards, those who had chosen to stay with Larus, fought with less discipline now, clearly unsettled by the turn of events. Their hold loosened around the perimeter. Tali's group of fighters had spread out among the quarry walls, and the soldiers now found them-selves trapped between the fighters in the middle and those on the wall.

Xiomara, who had worked tirelessly with Brindl on the catapult, now paused. "I'm afraid we might hurt our own people," she said, surveying the scene. The fighting had died down, and several soldiers put their hands up in surrender.

"Agreed," said Brindl. "Surely Larus will call off his

guards any minute now." She looked around the pit to locate the man, but he was nowhere to be seen. Nor was the former Queen.

"Brindl, quick!" someone said behind her, grabbing her shoulder.

"Tonio!" *Thank the Gods he's unharmed.*

"Twenty-two, Larus, Paulin . . . they've left the quarry through the western pass. We have to get to the palace before they do."

"But—" Brindl looked at Xia, then beyond her to the fight.

"I'll stay," Xiomara said, reading her thoughts. "I won't leave this quarry until the rest of our people are safe. You go. Find a way to stop Twenty-two, stop Larus, before they get to the palace grounds." Her glance flickered briefly on Tonio. "You know how vengeful they are. I would not see any more people hurt."

Brindl gave Xiomara a quick hug, then followed Tonio up a path out of the quarry. They walked quickly, almost at a trot, spilling tiny pebbles and pearldust down the steep, narrow passage.

Tonio led them away from the noise and smoke of Quarry Town to a wooded trail that paralleled the cart path to Fugaza. Quickly but quietly they made their way through the woods, taking cover in the thick brush. Before long, they spied Twenty-two and her small party—Larus, Paulin,

Ona—walking briskly along the cart path. Obviously, the horses they'd used to travel to Quarry Town were gone, perhaps spooked by the fire, or released by one of the villagers.

Now that the battle was behind them, the cold pressed into Brindl's clothes, and anger found her, too. The Diosa. The boy. Moth. How easily Larus had killed them all. How easily Twenty-two had stood by and let it happen. Brindl watched the once mighty Queen and her lady's maid struggle to stay upright on the uneven path, their delicate Moon Guilder shoes no match for the rugged landscape.

A group of Second Guard riders approached from around the curve. Tonio grabbed Brindl's hand and the two ducked behind a tree, blending into the landscape.

Brindl peered out from her hiding place and almost cried out in relief when she saw who it was.

Zarif. Chey. Jaden.

So Jaden is alive.

Brindl watched Twenty-two blanch upon seeing him, but recover just as quickly.

"Thank the Gods you're here!" she said. "The quarry workers are rioting. They've set their own town aflame!"

"How did this come to be?" Jaden demanded of Larus.

"It was an ambush. They tried to overthrow the Queen!"

"That's a lie!" Brindl cried, rushing out from the woods. "They're lying!"

Tonio emerged as well and stood beside Brindl. "Seize

Twenty-two," Tonio said. "Seize all of them! They've killed the Diosa. They've set fire to the quarry."

Jaden glanced quickly at Brindl, who nodded. "He speaks the truth."

Immediately, the three riders circled Twenty-two's party, creating a triangular barrier, their horses helping to form a blockade.

"Release us," demanded Paulin, his face nearly white with indignity. "I will not be treated as a prisoner here."

"Quiet," Jaden said, as Chey steered his horse in Paulin's direction, forcing the regent to scramble backward. Lady Ona, as usual, remained silent and stony-faced.

Brindl stepped forward then, face-to-face with Twenty-two. "This woman is no longer the Queen. The Diosa, last living Daughter of Machué, proclaimed Xiomara the rightful Queen of Tequende, before *he* put an arrow through the Diosa's heart," she said, pointing to Larus.

Across from her, she saw Chey's eyes widen. "He also ordered the Second Guard to execute innocent people. Thankfully, many of your guardsmen defected—those who had a *conscience*—to help the villagers. I believe the battle is nearly over. Xiomara—Queen Twenty-three—is down there now. Many are wounded. Some are dead."

"I suggest we take these people straight to the palace dungeon, Commander," said Zarif, his normally calm face filled with cold fury.

"Agreed," said Jaden.

Just then, Larus stepped behind Brindl and grabbed her in one swift motion. He pulled her against him, his blade pressed against her throat, before anyone could react.

Brindl felt her pulse beat against her like a drum.

"You will hand over your horses," Larus said, pressing the blade deeper, "or I will slice her to the bone."

"Unhand her, Larus. There's no need for more violence," Zarif said, looking at Brindl in alarm.

"The horses!" Larus demanded.

Zarif was the first to dismount, handing his horse to Twenty-two, though his eyes spit fire at her. Chey handed the reins of his horse to Lady Ona. As she threw a leg over the animal, her gown pulled up, revealing spindly legs with broken veins and a scar over her left knee. Even with a sword to her neck, Brindl couldn't help but notice how Lady Ona rushed to cover her legs, her vanity ever-present, though she'd just witnessed a bloody battle.

Finally, Paulin snatched the reins from Jaden's hands and hastily jumped into the saddle. They galloped off without a backward glance, as Centurio Larus remained behind, his sword still at Brindl's neck.

"Release her," demanded Jaden. "You have what you want now."

Larus backed away slowly, keeping his eyes trained on the soldiers. "I'll do no such thing, for she is my ticket to freedom."

No I am not, thought Brindl, slowly reaching a hand under her tunic.

In one quick movement, she pulled out the dagger from Lord Yonda and plunged it straight into Larus's thigh. The centurio staggered as Tonio burst from the side of the road and bashed a chunk of pearlstone onto the back of Larus's head.

The centurio collapsed to the ground, his sword clattering on the road.

(If you happen to be reading this tiresome book, may I suggest instead The Rise of Tequende: A History by M. de Saavedra, with revisions by Z. B. Hasan, to truly understand the hard-won glories of our realm —B. T.)

This training manual, commissioned by ~~the wise and magnanimous~~ Queen Twenty-two, should be kept on hand at all times by every servant and attendant to the Crown, for the glory of our realm depends upon obedience.

—Ch. N. Tasca, *Palace Etiquette*

TWENTY-FIVE

rindl sat at the western edge of the palace, perched on top of the storage trunk. She settled into the best spot with the widest view of Fugaza through the battlements and pulled Pip out of her pocket. The bird peeped quietly as if he didn't wish to disturb Brindl's slice of peace.

"How good it is to see you, my little friend." She stroked the top of his head, just as he liked, and he rewarded her with friendly pecks to the palm. Brindl knew the stolen moment wouldn't last, but she'd hoped to have a few minutes more before she heard the chamberlain's heavy steps approach. Two months ago, Brindl would've rushed to right herself and look presentable, but now she stayed on her cozy roost and acknowledged the woman with a nod.

"Lady Brindl," the chamberlain began, gesturing to the tower room.

"Just Brindl, please."

"Yes, well . . ." The chamberlain paused, obviously struggling to adapt to her new role with someone who had once—and not that long ago—been leagues below her in rank. "*Brindl*, Lili has gone to gather her things. She'll begin sharing the tower rooms with you tonight."

"Yes, very good," Brindl said, smiling at the thought of sharing her space with the little charmer.

"It's just . . . Would you not prefer more comfortable quarters in the palace?"

"I would not, thank you just the same."

"But"—the chamberlain hesitated again, searching for words—"is it not *unseemly* for a person in your new position—Counselor to the Queen—to share quarters with a pigeonkeep?"

"Ah, yes, unseemly. That reminds me . . ." Brindl stood and walked to the tower, motioning for the chamberlain to follow. Inside, she pulled a book off her shelves. "Here it is. *Palace Etiquette*. I don't believe I'll be needing it any longer," she said cheerfully, handing it over.

"What about Lili?" the Chamberlain asked.

"No need! She'll catch on quick; she's bright as a button."

The chamberlain took the book and frowned. "I'll be leaving, then."

A most excellent decision, Brindl thought, though she held her tongue.

Not long after the chamberlain left, Brindl heard a knock at the door.

"Come in, Zarif," she called. Often of late he'd made a habit of finding her at the end of the day for a cup of chocolate and a chat.

Zarif followed her companionably into the kitchen, where the chocolate was already waiting, warm on dark coals. She poured the cups and carried them out to the roof, the familiar crunch of Zarif's wooden crutches on the stony surface beside her.

"Did I tell you about Ory's decision?" Brindl began, handing Zarif a cup once he'd settled onto the trunk.

"What did our little hero decide?" Zarif asked, taking a sip of the hot beverage.

Brindl smiled. Ory was a hero, after all. He'd led dozens of families to safety during the battle of the quarry, including many young children. For his bravery, Xiomara had offered him a position at the palace, but he preferred to stay in the mines. *Too many Toppers up top,* he'd said with his funny grin. *Besides, we have a whole new batch of firsties who don't know their pick from their axe!*

Brindl chuckled, remembering the conversation. "Ory promises to visit, but he prefers to stay in the mines. He plans to train the first-year miners, as I once did." She placed Pip on top of the battlement between them where he hopped around and picked at the small pebbles, looking for something to eat. "He was heartbroken over the loss of the Diosa, of course."

"A needless tragedy," Zarif said, shaking his head. He reached out his finger and Pip jumped onto the perch, then off again.

"Yes." Brindl paused. She'd thought a great deal about her last conversation with the Diosa; in fact, she had played it over and again in her mind. "But I think she knew it was going to happen . . . that she was going to die at the quarry."

"Truly?" Zarif stopped petting Pip and looked directly at Brindl. She'd forgotten how golden his eyes were, almost the same color as Intiq's fading light.

"Truly. She said if she ever left the mines she'd never return. And then she asked, 'Is it time?' I was so distraught and confused, I didn't understand the significance of her question then. But I'm the one that told her yes, Zarif. That it *was* time."

"But you didn't kill her, Brin. You can't hold yourself responsible for that. That lands squarely on Larus's shoulders, no one else's. And he'll spend the rest of his life in a dungeon for it," Zarif added, though it wasn't much consolation for either of them.

"Is he still claiming that Twenty-two was innocent of all wrongdoing?" Brindl asked.

Zarif nodded. "Still blindly loyal. According to him,

Twenty-two was poorly advised by those who would abuse her power, namely Ona, and then Paulin. He says Ona planned to get rid of Xiomara so she herself would become Queen-in-Waiting."

"The chandelier!" Brindl cried, putting the pieces together. "That was Ona?"

"Most likely," Zarif answered, leaning forward to watch the sun slide past the Sentry Hills. "Though we may never know. Rumor has it that Ona, Paulin, and Twenty-two have boarded a ship to the Far World."

"The farther, the better," Brindl said, "though I'm surprised they didn't take exile closer to home to plot their revenge."

"Apparently, Twenty-two is afraid the Shadow Guard wants her head for the destruction of Quarry Town. Meanwhile, Paulin's Blood Queen, Beatríz, has offered them asylum."

Brindl shivered as a breeze came down the mountains, and she scooped Pip into her pocket. "They deserve each other. But the Shadow Guard leaders would not seek revenge, I'm certain of that. They've agreed to stand down, and the talks with Xia have gone well. They have enormous respect for her. And trust."

"Thanks to you," Zarif said.

"Thanks to both sides. I'm just the intermediary. A messenger bird."

Brindl stood then and moved the few steps toward the battlements to see the last bit of sun brighten the Magda River. It looked like a golden snake slithering through the green valley. A quiet blanketed the scene, as workers moved inside for the evening meal with friends and family.

Zarif joined her at the battlement. "You're more than a messenger. All along you saw what I could not see. I'm sorry it's taken me this long to realize how small my view of Tequende was, how much I chose to overlook. I have much to learn from you, Brindl. Will you forgive me?"

"Of course," she answered, turning toward him. "And I have much to learn from you, Zarif Baz Hasan. History, politics, economics, what to feed Lord Yonda during his visit next month . . ."

Zarif smiled. "We'll teach each other, then," he said, placing his hand on hers.

"I like that idea."

"We're here!" sang Tali, from across the roof.

"And we have a cake!" called Chey.

"Mama Rossi made you the one with honey, Brin," Tonio added. "Your favorite!"

Brindl and Zarif shared one last smile, then turned to greet their friends.

May every evening be this lovely, thought Brindl.

And may this be the first of thousands.

My dearest Brindl,

I'm finally taking a moment on the balcony to
write you a letter, much overdue. It is a perfect
afternoon, so I decided my desk in the library could
spare an hour without me. A slice of sunshine has
found me, and I feel like a cat sunning myself,
listening to the great Magda rush below. I promised
to catch you up on our news, so I must endeavor to
do so.

The Queen's Library has expanded under
Zarif's keen direction and he has devised a way
for any citizen of the realm to borrow a book. Of
course, he makes them sign in blood that—should
calamity befall them—they will save the book
before themselves, their belongings, and even their
offspring! I've allocated a large budget for his
acquisitions and less for glinting objects from the
Far World, though I have commissioned several
sculptures from Tonio Rossi, of which I think you
will approve. Quarry Town has been completely
rebuilt, and soon the town square will be wreathed
in monuments to the Diosa, Moth, and all those
who fell during battle, may the Mother hold them. I

do hope you'll be able to join us for the unveiling.

A fortnight ago Tali and Jaden returned to report on the state of our borders to the north. Tali is much improved in disposition with her new responsibilities. After several nights here, they commenced their journey west, and then they will head south to the Alcazar for the next round of recruits. Jaden, too, seemed in high spirits and I do suspect their happiness is a direct result of their proximity to each other.

Chey is standing mere feet away, even as I write this. He is so protective of me as the Palace Centurio and I am much indebted to him. With him, I fear not the future nor my path in it. Since the unrest in the quarry he will not be swayed to part from me, and in truth, my dear friend, I do not want him to.

Now, despite my delay in responding, I hope you will offer me a detailed letter telling me all of the news from Zipa. How much longer until you can invite children inside the Saavedra Academy for Learning? How proud our tutor would be to know of this tribute! The crates of books that will help you with your endeavors should be arriving soon.

Zarif curated the collection himself and I think you will be pleased. The academy in Quarry Town opened last month and the children and parents are delighted with it!

I'm sorry that I cannot write more, but I must meet with Lord Yonda soon. He's brought his whole family this time—what a passel of children and grandchildren that man has!—which has kept the chamberlain on her toes, as you might imagine!

Zarif, Chey, Tonio, and I look forward to your next visit, so please don't keep us waiting much longer. The palace rooftop isn't the same without you.

Yours,
Xia

ACKNOWLEDGMENTS

Our deepest gratitude to:

Kevin Lewis, for taking the chance.

Ricardo Mejías, for taking the helm.

Barry Goldblatt, for getting us started.

Tracey and Josh Adams, for seeing us through.

The Disney-Hyperion gang, for ongoing support, and Kelley McMorris, for the gorgeous covers!

Team JD: Heartfelt thanks to Tracie Vaughn Kleman, for her poet's eye, pretty words, and good humor throughout the many pages of our friendship. To Kevin Lewis, for constantly inspiring us with his Ory-like enthusiasm, Zarif-like curiosity, and Tali-like courage. And to Ricardo Mejías, our own young Saavedra, for his endless patience, wise insights, and for seeing the forest when we could only see trees. It was an honor to share the world of Tequende with you. Boundless appreciation as well to the people who keep me tethered to the real world with their love and loyalty. My family: Kyle and Ryan Durango; Larry and Susan Greider; Sherry, Natalie, Hillary, and Chad Stanford. My Westside family: Diane and Bill Stevenson; Angie, Mike, Jack, and Bridget Stevenson; Katie, Joe, Joey, and Will Trupiano. And, of course, my True Blues: Bill Cairns, Jenny Cottingham, Peter Kousathanas, Catalina Malaver, Juliana Parra, Doris Samuelson, and Tyler Terrones.

Team TVZ: To Gary Kleman, a man who defines so many words for this writer: love, devotion, compassion, patience, and honor. To our awesome pack of kids who paint every single day with the brightest colors: Cole and Abbie Zimmer; Gryphon and Teagan Kleman. My mom and bonus dad: Pauline and Werner Schwitalski, for always listening. My twin sister, Trish DeLong, for shenanigans and our big brother, Paul Vaughn, for getting us out of them. To my nieces and nephews, I love you all so much: Zach, Mahaley, and Jesse Vaughn; Wes, Alec, and Josie DeLong; Chase and Reagan Schwitalski. To the whole Kleman clan for such a warm welcome into the fold: Jackie and Ray, Steve, Becky, and Nick Kleman; Diane, Al, and Erick Starkey; Sarah and Donny Westcamp; Jody, Pete, Jackie, and Zach Bible; Jeff and Rachel Holstein; Jamey and Aunt Kay Harker. A huge bow to the Disney gang for making so many dreams come true: Kevin Lewis, Ricardo Mejías, Joann Hill, and Dina Sherman. I'm fortunate to have dear friends who guide me in writing and life: Laura Collier, Jessica Swaim, Mary Mahoney, Amanda Bimonte, and Patty Piron. Buckets of gratitude, love, and friendship to my writing partner, Julia Durango, who has taught me how to plot stories and a life I love—we made it, JJ!